THE ICE HARVEST

THE ICE

SCOTT PHILLIPS

HARVEST

PICADOR

First published 2000 by Picador
an imprint of Macmillan Publishers Ltd
25 Eccleston Place, London SW1W 9NF
Basingstoke and Oxford
Associated companies throughout the world
www.macmillan.com

ISBN 0 330 48137 1

9 8 7 6 5 4 3 2 1

A CIP catalogue record for this book is available from
the British Library.

Typeset by SetSystems Ltd, Saffron Walden, Essex
Printed and bound in Great Britain by
Mackays of Chatham plc, Chatham, Kent

To Anne, with all my love

WICHITA, KANSAS. CHRISTMAS EVE 1979

PART ONE

CHAPTER ONE

At four-fifteen on a cold, dry Christmas Eve a nervous middle-aged man in an expensive overcoat walked bareheaded into the Midtown Tap Room and stood at the near end of the bar with his membership card in hand, waiting for the afternoon barmaid to get off the phone. She was about forty, heavy in a square way, with a shiny face and dishwater blonde hair that looked like she'd got shitfaced and decided to cut it herself. He knew she'd noticed him coming in, but she was taking great pains to pretend she couldn't see him. To do so she had to stand at a peculiar angle, leaning her hip against the back bar and looking off toward the back door so that she was facing neither the lawyer nor the mirror behind her.

The only other drinker at that hour was a small, very slender young man in a fully buttoned jean jacket who sat leaning his elbow on the bar, his cheek resting on the heel of his wrist with a cigarette between his index and middle fingers, its ash end burning dangerously close to the tip of his oily pompadour. His eyes were closed and his mouth open.

The lawyer unbuttoned his overcoat and stood there

for a minute, listening to the barmaid's phone conversation. She had just the start of a drinker's rasp, and if he was just hearing her on the phone and not looking at her he'd have thought it sounded sexy. She seemed to be having some kind of roommate trouble involving a fender bender, a borrowed car and no insurance, and it didn't look as though she'd be noticing him anytime soon.

He couldn't remember ever seeing the Tap Room in daylight before, if the failing grey light filtering through the grime on the front windows qualified as such. It was a deep, narrow old building with a battered pressed-tin ceiling and a long oak bar. On the brick wall behind the bandstand hung a huge blackfaced clock with fluorescent purple numbers, and running the length of the opposite wall was a row of red Naugahyde booths. All of this was festooned with cheap plastic holly and mistletoe. Around the walls seven feet or so from the floor ran a string of multicolored Christmas lights, unplugged at the moment. This is my last look at this place, he thought, mildly surprised at the idea. He hadn't been out of town for more than two or three days at a time in fifteen years.

A squeal from the barmaid interrupted his reverie. 'Jesus Christ, Gary, you set your hair on fire!' Young Gary looked up in cross-eyed bewilderment at the hiss of the wet rag she was patting against his smoldering forelock. He protested weakly and unintelligibly as she snatched his cigarette away from him and ground it out in the ashtray, then put the ashtray behind the bar. 'It's obvious you can't be trusted with these any more,' she said as she confiscated his cigarettes and lighter. He started to say something in his own defense, but stopped and closed his eyes again, resting his cheek back down on his hands. 'You'll get these back tomorrow,' she said. 'You want another drink?' Gary nodded yes without opening his eyes.

Now she looked up at the newcomer, feigning surprise. 'Oh, hi. Didn't see you come in.' She gave his membership card a perfunctory glance. 'What can I get you?'

'C.C. Waterback.' She turned without a word and busied herself making his drink, following it with another for Gary. 'Is Tommy in back?' the man said as she set the drinks down.

'Nope. He'll be in tonight.'

'Could you give him this for me?' He handed her an envelope.

'Sure,' she said. She took the envelope from his hand and turned it over a couple of times as though looking for a set of instructions.

'Tell him it's from Charlie Arglist.'

'Charlie Arglist?' There was genuine surprise in her voice this time. She lowered her head, cocking it to one side, giving him a close look. 'Charlie, is that you?'

'Yeah . . .' At that moment he was certain he'd never seen the woman before in his life.

'Jesus, Charlie, it's me, Susie Tannenger. Wow, have you ever changed.' She stepped back to let him get a better look at her. The Susie Tannenger he remembered was a lithe, pretty thing, at least six or eight years younger than he was. He had handled a divorce for her about ten years earlier, and in the course of the proceedings her husband, a commercial pilot, had threatened several times to kill Charlie.

She came around the bar and gave him a hug, a hard one with a discreet little pelvic bump thrown in. Her ex had had good reason to want to kill him; he had taken out his fee in trade, at her suggestion, on his desktop.

'Isn't life funny? Are you still a lawyer? Hey, Gary, check it out – this is the guy that did my first divorce!'

Gary looked up, focused for a split second, then grunted and returned to his private ruminations.

'Charlie, this is my fiancé, Gary. Shit, I didn't even know you were still in town, we gotta get together sometime.'

'Yeah, we should do that.' Charlie knocked back his drink and set a five-dollar bill on the table. 'Well, I got some Christmas shopping left to do. Nice to see you again, Susie.'

She swept up the bill and handed it back to him. 'Your money's no good here, counselor. Merry Christmas!'

'Thanks, Susie. Same to you.' He went to the door. It was getting dark outside, and Susie hadn't yet turned the overhead lights on. From that distance, in that dim, smoky light, he almost recognized her. 'And a Happy New Year to you both,' he said as he pushed the door open and stepped out onto the ice.

When the door closed Susie sighed and looked over at Gary, whose head had migrated down to the bar and who had started to snore. 'There goes the second most inconsiderate lay I ever had,' she said.

*

Who gives a shit if I say goodbye to Tommy or not anyway, Charlie thought. He was warm and dry behind the wheel of the company car, a brand new black 1980 Lincoln Continental, the finest car he had ever driven. He was headed west with no particular destination in mind. It was dark and overcast, one of those days where it was impossible to tell whether the sun was still up or not, but as yet it hadn't started to snow. He passed the Hardee's across the street from Grove High, watched the kids hanging around in the parking lot the way he had when he was in school, back when it had been a Sandy's. His kids wouldn't go to Grove, close as they lived to it; they'd be assigned to one of the newer and presumably nicer schools further east. Good for them, fuck all this nostalgia crap. He pulled a flask from the inside pocket of his overcoat and took a long drink. Now might be a good time to stop by the Sweet Cage; the afternoon shift would be ending, and there were a couple of the daytime dancers he wanted to see one last time. It was a little after four-thirty, and he had nine and a half hours to kill.

*

Charlie had both hands resting on top of the wheel, trying to screw the cap back on the flask, when he caught sight of a police cruiser just behind him to the left, gaining slowly. He quickly gripped the steering wheel with his left hand and lowered the flask in his right, spilling a little bourbon on his pant's leg.

'Ah, shit . . .' He looked down at the stain, just to the right of his crotch. 'Looks like I pissed my fucking pants.' He looked up as he felt the car swerve, catching it at the last possible moment and swinging back into the right-hand lane. The black and white pulled up alongside him and Charlie looked calmly over. The cop on the right rolled his window down and Charlie did the same.

'Road sure is icy, counselor,' the cop shouted, his face pinched against the cold wind.

'Sure is, officer.' He tried to remember the cop's name.

'You're doing forty in a school zone, you know.'

'Shit. Sorry.' Charlie let his foot up off the gas, and the cops slowed down with him.

'Never know who's gonna clock you around here, Mister Arglist.'

'Thanks. That's one I owe you.'

'Merry Christmas.'

'Merry Christmas, guys.' He held up the flask and drank them a short toast and they accelerated away, laughing and waving. That was a lucky fucking break, he thought. He switched on the AM radio and rolled the tuner knob between thumb and forefinger until he found an adenoidal police reporter giving quick but detailed accounts of a fistfight in a tavern, a foiled daylight burglary and a rash of car thefts at a local shopping mall. He closed his report with a message from the Chief of Police admonishing shoppers to lock their cars and take their keys. He was followed by an equally adenoidal country singer's bland, stringy rendition of 'On the First Noël'. Charlie took another sip and wondered who the hell burgled in the daytime, on Christmas Eve yet.

CHAPTER TWO

It was slow going at the Sweet Cage; the after-five office crowd were all at home tonight with their families or getting hammered at office parties. Besides Charlie, only a handful of sullen college kids and a retired postal worker named Culligan were on hand to appreciate the artistry of Rusti, a pudgy, redheaded twenty-year-old with a black eye and a Farrah Fawcett-Majors hairdo. A crude, bluish tattoo of a bird flitted above her left nipple and the words 'FREE BIRD' encircled her right as she danced to her usual slow, languorous rhythm, pointedly ignoring as always the tempo of the song on the jukebox. She held her elbows out to her sides and moved them back and forth in a crawling motion, her hips rotating in counterpoint, head nodding arrhythmically, eyes vacant. Charlie asked her about the glazed look once, and she explained that as soon as her bra and panties fell to the stage and no further concentration was called for she entered into a trance state during which she communicated with the dead and could no longer hear the music to dance to it. Charlie had nodded gravely, politely declining her offer to contact any of his dear departed.

One of the college boys, a kid in a sheepskin coat and hiking boots, stared at her churning on the tiny, circular stage with a particular sad intensity, seemingly about to cry.

Charlie watched him from the bar, wondering if he was a rejected swain. The bartender, a large popeyed man with unkempt, curly black hair, also had a watchful eye on the boy. 'Who gave her the black eye, Sidney?' Charlie asked.

'Her asshole boyfriend did it two days ago. I wanted to break his fucking hands. She begged me not to, said he was real sorry, and how it'd never happen again, all that shit. Said she loves him.'

'Jesus, that's too bad.'

'I'm still gonna break his hands, Charlie, swear to Christ.'

'Is it that kid staring at her?'

'No, that's just some kid, says he went to high school with her. The boyfriend's a skinny little fucker, thinks he's gonna be a big rock star.' Sidney banged out a chord on an imaginary guitar.

'Hence the breaking of the hands, rather than the legs or arms.'

'You got it. You know how many bones there are in the human hand?'

'Not off the top of my head.'

'Me neither, but I'm gonna break all of 'em.'

The office door opened and a tall woman in a charcoal grey pinstriped suit and black heels stepped behind the bar. Her hair was black with a few wisps of grey, tied into a severe bun at the back of her long neck, and her face was untouched by laugh lines. Her exact age and origins had been the subject of idle speculation for years; she might have been thirty-five or fifty-five, and her accent was so mild and Americanized that it was impossible to pin it down to a specific country. Charlie had heard arguments for French Canada, Greece, Czechoslovakia, Brazil, Russia and Portugal, none of them any better thought out than random stabs in the dark.

She looked out at the sparse crowd and shook her head. 'People think because it's Christmas all of a sudden they can't look at tits and ass.'

Sidney nodded. 'God and Santa Claus, they're both watching.'

She came around the bar and took a seat next to Charlie, spreading some legal documents in front of her. Sidney handed her a bottle of beer. 'Hi, Charlie.'

'Hi, Renata. How's it going?'

'Shitty.' She kept her eyes on the papers, tight-lipped and squinting. 'I may have to move the club outside the city.'

'Really?'

'Either that or put G-strings on the girls, or quit serving beer. I don't see any way around it now. Looks like there's going to be no nude dancing in beer taverns inside the city limits.'

Sidney slammed his fist down on the bar hard enough that everyone in the room jumped except for Rusti, whose adagio mingling with the Beyond continued uninterrupted. 'It sucks!'

Renata patted his shoulder soothingly, without looking particularly sympathetic.

'Fucking town's turning into a real shithole. I'm about ready to leave, I really am.'

He folded his solid arms across his chest, scowling and petulant. 'We've always done good business out in the county,' Charlie offered as consolation.

'Yeah, but you don't get the downtowners after work, do you?' Renata said. 'That's my bread-and-butter trade. What the hell kind of tippers do you get out in the county? Your girls can barely pay their stage rentals. Shit, I may have to try putting G-strings on 'em, see if it really does slow things down.'

Sidney's fury had not abated. 'Bullshit! People come in here, they want to see pussy and drink beer! G-strings and soda pop, my ass.'

Renata shrugged. 'Yeah,' she admitted, 'pussy is what they want, all right.' She looked at the papers spread out on the bar and sighed.

'I don't know, I'd say you've got at least two potential swing votes on the commission. It's not a lost cause yet.'

'Yes, it is. And there's no swing vote, believe me. I've tried hard with both of them. We're stuck.'

'Maybe so.' It wasn't of any practical concern to him at this point, but he hated to see Renata backed up against the wall.

'Wish I could get my hands on that picture of yours, Charlie.'

'Which picture?' Charlie said.

'You know goddamn well which picture. Trouble is, Bill Gerard has no sense of solidarity.'

Sidney snorted. 'That's a picture I'd like to see on the front page of the morning paper,' he said.

Charlie leaned into the bar, an idea starting to take form. What did it matter what happened to the photo, once he was gone? It was one more way to fuck Deacon and Bill Gerard and the whole bunch of them, let them wake up Christmas morning and find that their ace in the hole had vanished along with Charlie and Vic and everything else.

'Sidney, I'm buying the counselor's beer tonight,' Renata said. She got up from her stool and moved behind Charlie, placing her hands on his shoulders, her long, sculptured red nails pressing through the fabric of his coat and shirt. Blood surged instantly to his groin and his scalp began to tingle, and he felt more warm blood gathering itself in his cheeks. She gave him a couple of affectionate squeezes, and he was sure she was reading his mind. 'Talk to you later, Charlie.' She walked away from the bar, toward the front door. 'Back in a couple hours,' she called out to Sidney without looking back. With the sole exception of Rusti's heartbroken classmate, the attention of every male in the room was riveted on the movement of Renata's pinstriped hips. There had never been a dancer at the Sweet Cage who came within shouting distance of Renata's league, and no one Charlie knew had ever seen her remove so much as her suit jacket.

When the door closed behind her with a muffled thud they all watched it for a moment, then reluctantly turned their attentions back to Rusti or to their beers, looking as if they had just awakened from a pleasant but unrealizable dream. Culligan, his attention span shortened by years of daytime drinking, was the first to recover, and he applauded wildly as the song on the jukebox ended and Rusti returned to the land of the living. 'Give her a tip, boys, she puts on a good show,' he cried, his voice cracking with delight. Gleefully he reached into his breast pocket and handed Rusti a ten, which she placed into a highball glass on the edge of the stage. 'Come on, fellers, don't be stingy. She puts on a hell of a show.' A couple of the college boys reluctantly pulled out their wallets and started thumbing through their cash supplies. The boy in the sheepskin coat continued to mope, glaring now at Culligan. 'See that there?' Culligan continued. 'That's a redhead snatch, that's the real thing. Ain't no dye job on Rusti, nosirreebob, that there's one hundred percent natural red hair pie.' This was the old man's natural redhead variant on the standard spiel he gave after every dancer finished; Rusti didn't seem to be hearing it, but the look on the boy's face moved from loving despair to murderous rage. Culligan licked his upper lip with an obscene slurping sound, his watery eyes shining dementedly. 'You ain't never tasted no snatch like that one, I'll guarantee you—'

The boy rose from his chair with something between a sob and a war cry and leapt onto Culligan, whose chair gave under him with an audible crack. 'Shut up, shut up,' the boy sobbed over and over.

'Fuck,' Sidney said, reaching down for his baseball bat. Charlie moved to one side to allow him to vault over the bar and the big man strode across the room, thumping the bat into his left hand. Rusti looked down on the scene in horror. 'Donny!' she yelled. 'Quit it! Get up off of him!' Donny seemed not to hear her. His comrades rose up nervously as if to come to his aid, but a glance from Sidney was enough to get them moving backwards and away from the struggle.

'I'm a cripple, I'm a cripple,' the old man howled, 'don't hurt me!' In fact Donny was just holding him down in a bear hug, and Charlie almost felt sorry for the lad when he heard the impact of the bat on his knee. The boy screamed in pain and shock and rolled off of Culligan and lay there holding the knee, wide-eyed and breathless. Culligan, realizing that he was essentially undamaged, sat down in another chair.

'Sidney, stop! That's enough!' Rusti cried from the stage. Donny looked up for a moment at her, heartened by this show of compassion from his beloved, and then the bat caught him on the right shin, at which point Rusti jumped down from the stage and threw herself over him, weeping. 'Donny, Donny, did he hurt you?'

Breathing hard, Sidney leaned jauntily on the bat like a cricket player. 'Fuckin'-A I hurt him.'

The three boys who were still standing started to move for the door. 'Hey,' Sidney barked, straightening up and extending the bat towards them. They froze where they stood, terrified. He swung the bat in the direction of the highball glass with its lone ten-dollar bill. 'Tip the lady.' They stepped dutifully forward and around their fallen comrade, and each stuffed a couple of dollars into the glass before heading once again for the door. 'You don't have to leave, boys,' Culligan cried out, his short-term memory too feeble to hold much of a grudge. 'Stick around for Amy Sue's number, she'll get you good and hot.'

'Yeah,' Sidney said. 'Stick around. Your buddy's gonna have to wait outside, though.' Donny still lay on the floor, weeping in Rusti's arms.

'Donny, Donny . . .' She cradled him gently, brushing his hair with her short fingers. 'Poor little Donny baby.' He said something nobody could make out. 'What? I can't hear you.'

He spoke up. 'Ronny,' he said. 'My name's Ronny.'

Amy Sue, a skinny brunette in shiny blue bikini panties and matching bra, was punching up tunes on the jukebox. She looked over the room, only mildly discouraged at the size of the audience. Her first song came on and she climbed onto the stage and started to dance.

'All right,' Sidney said, tapping Ronny's hiking boot with the tip of the bat. 'Time to go, pal.'

'Come on, Ronny,' Rusti said. 'We'll go sit in my car while your buddies watch Amy Sue.' She helped him to his feet and covered herself with the robe Amy Sue had just removed, then she took the sheepskin coat from her unsteady, blubbering champion and put it on. He didn't seem to notice, overwhelmed simultaneously by the pain in his knees and by the unexpected attention of his feminine ideal. She accompanied him outside and his friends shrugged and sat back down. They still had most of a pitcher of beer left.

Sidney got back behind the bar and set a fresh beer down in front of Charlie. 'Jesus H. Christ,' he said, 'what's next?'

Despite his earlier endorsement, Culligan found himself losing interest in Amy Sue and he limped over to Charlie, bracing himself on the scuffed Formica tables as he passed them. 'Any chance you might be heading out to the 'Rama tonight, Charlie?'

An hour ago there hadn't been, but now there was the matter of getting the photo out of Bill Gerard's hands and into Renata's. 'Yeah, I guess I'm heading out there now. You need a ride?'

Culligan's head bobbed idiotically. 'Sure do.'

Charlie swigged his fresh beer down to the foam and slid off his barstool. 'I'll be back later,' he told Sidney.

'Bring some customers back with you,' Sidney said. 'We're not gonna make shit tonight.'

'I will,' he said. Amy Sue stared after them as they headed for the door, hurt that they were taking off in the middle of her act. Neither Charlie nor Culligan gave her a second thought on their way out.

CHAPTER THREE

'I believe that boy hurt me.' Tiny specks of saliva flew from Culligan's lips onto the passenger window as he spoke. He held his crooked left arm straight out to his side, letting it swing to and fro from the elbow like a pendulum, coming perilously close to Charlie's right arm with each swing. 'This arm hasn't been right since '43.'

'War?'

'Aw, fuck no, I wasn't in the war. Hockey. See, all the aircraft plants had teams, we used to play out at the ice rink Sundays. A lot of fellas stateside felt like they had something to prove, figured everybody took 'em for 4-F or queer or yellow, so we ended up fighting more than playing. I don't imagine there was ever anybody in the crowd came wanting to watch any hockey.'

'I remember. My dad took me to a couple games, I must have been about six or seven. Tail end of the war.'

'Well, sir, that's what happened to my arm and my hip, and I got a trick knee too you could probably put down to a time this fatass welder body-checked me right into the side of the rink. I went after him with my stick, damn near put out his eye.' The old man smiled placidly, savoring the memory.

Snow had started to come down lightly and the county road was dark, the streetlamps few and far between. There was no traffic heading north away from town, and Charlie knew the club would be empty. One last chance for him to listen to the dancers piss and moan about how slow it was, as though Christmas were something he'd dreamed up himself just to fuck them over.

Beside him Culligan recited a litany of all the drunken insults his body had endured over the years: concussions, dislocations, broken bones, a third-degree burn on his good arm. Nearly all of these were directly or indirectly self-inflicted; Rusti's young admirer was far from the first drunk Culligan had goaded into felonious assault.

'You ever been married, Charlie?'

'What?'

'I said you ever been married?'

'Yeah . . .'

'Then you know what I'm talking about. Deadlier than the male. See this here—' Culligan pointed to a jagged, narrow strip of smooth pink skin that neatly bisected his left eyebrow and ran another inch up his forehead. 'Another half-inch down I woulda lost the eye.'

'Your wife did that?'

'She sure as hell did. Gave her what for, too.'

'You hit her?'

Culligan was appalled. 'I never hit a woman my whole damn life. Christ, what the hell you take me for?'

Charlie shrugged. 'Sorry.'

'Fuck no, I walked out on her, left her with two school-age kids to support.'

'Didn't know you had kids.'

'Sure. Her two, plus another girl, she's about your age. None of 'em'll have anything to do with me now. Their mothers' poisoned 'em against me.'

'Sorry.'

'Hell, I don't care. Some of us just wasn't made to be dads.' He was silent for a moment. 'Do you know if Cupcake's dancing tonight?'

*

As they pulled into the parking lot Charlie noted, point-lessly now, that the neon sign needed repair again. The dancing girl's white go-go boots were both dark, and so were the T and the O in 'Tease-O-Rama'. There were three cars in the lot. 'Looks like you're gonna get a show all to yourself,' Charlie said. The snow was coming down a little harder now.

Inside, one of the dancers was shrieking at the bartender, who looked up at Charlie and Culligan's arrival. The dancer paid them no mind.

'Fuck working Christmas for no money!' She had on a shiny gold G-string and nothing else. 'I'm not gonna operate at a loss on a goddamn holiday! I could be at home enjoying Christmas Eve with my kids!'

'Your husband's got your kids, Francie,' the bartender reminded her in a gentle, monotonous baritone. 'They're in Denver.'

'Fuck you for throwing that in my face, Dennis.' She sat down on a stool and started crying.

'Now, come on, Francie, it's not so bad. See? Culligan's here.'

Francie looked up, wet-eyed, at Culligan and Charlie. Culligan was overjoyed at the sight of her. 'Howdy, Francie. Like your new hairdo.' She had on the same wig she always wore, long black curls that fell halfway down her back. Charlie had known her for ten years and had no idea what her real hair looked like. As far as he knew she might have been completely bald under there.

She ignored Culligan and unloaded on Charlie. 'You heard what I told Dennis. I'm not going on. Fuck paying you a twenty-five dollar stage rental, I'll be lucky to make ten tonight.'

Culligan was hurt. 'You know I'm good for twenty, Francie.'

'That still puts me five bucks in the hole. Fuck paying Bill Gerard five bucks for the privilege of letting that randy old pervert stare up my twat all night.'

Charlie sighed. The old speech, one last time. He'd made it a thousand times in six or seven years, probably a hundred of those to Francie alone. 'Francie, you can't just work the nights you want. You want to work the hot nights you gotta work the cold. You miss a scheduled night without a goddamn good reason, you lose your spot. Understand?'

'I understand it's Christmas Eve, there's nobody *in* here, and I still gotta pay a twenty-five dollar stage rental even though there's nobody to fucking dance for!'

Culligan's voice was thick with hurt and desire. 'I'm here,' he choked.

'Go on, Francie, dance for old Culligan,' Dennis droned from behind the bar.

She turned back to him in a fury. 'I already told you, even if he gives me twenty I'm still five in the hole!'

'I could make it twenty-five, sweetie,' Culligan whimpered.

'And I'm still dancing for free!'

Charlie held up his hand. 'Tell you what, Francie. It's Christmas Eve. If you'll go on, your stage rental's on the house.'

Francie was stunned into an unaccustomed momentary silence. Dennis raised an appraising eyebrow at Charlie, then turned back to his bar inventory. Culligan pressed forward and took Francie by the hand and led her toward one of the tiny stages. She looked back at Charlie, uncertain exactly how to interpret the gesture. 'Thanks, Charlie,' she said.

'So what makes you such a friend to the working girl all of a sudden?' Dennis set a beer down on the bar in front of Charlie, then turned and flicked the PA system on.

'Merry Christmas, Dennis.' He picked up the beer and took a long pull at it. On the small stage, Francie had begun dancing for an enraptured Culligan to a syrupy pop song. 'Who else is here?'

'Cupcake. She's in the office. Told her I'd yell if anyone showed up.'

'She pay her stage rental yet?'

'Course she did.'

'Give it to me.'

Dennis looked skeptical, then turned to the cash register. 'You clear this with Vic?'

'Don't have to. I'll cover it myself if I have to.'

Dennis handed him two tens and a five. 'I don't think that's the point, Charles. I think it's the precedent you're setting.'

'It's Christmas Eve, Dennis. God's birthday.' He walked back toward the office with Cupcake's refund. Francie had already dropped her G-string and she crouched awkwardly, concentrating hard, trying to take a five-dollar bill from Culligan's palsied hand with her labia.

*

Cupcake sat in a shiny gold bikini at Charlie's desk reading a paperback biography of Gandhi, swiveling the chair in listless semicircles to the time of the music outside. She barely looked up as Charlie walked in.

'I suppose the music means we got customers.'

'Just Culligan. Here.' Charlie handed her the money.

'What the fuck is this, my Christmas bonus?'

'It's your stage rental. It's on the house tonight.'

She looked skeptically down at the bills in her hand, then shrugged and put the money in her purse. 'I can always use twenty-five bucks. Thanks.' She frowned. 'I saw Desiray's kids this morning.'

Charlie swallowed. 'Where?'

'They're staying over at her sister's house. I brought them each a little present.'

'Kids okay?'

'How could they be? Jesus, Charlie. I don't think the

sister's too worried about Desiray, either. Good riddance, far as she's concerned.'

Charlie wasn't eager to think about Desiray. 'Well, she'll turn up eventually.'

'Oh, yeah, sure she will. Just like Santa's gonna be coming down the chimney tonight.'

Charlie coughed a little, trying to dislodge a speck of itchy phlegm from his throat. He was trying not to glance too obviously at the safe. 'Why don't you go to the bar and tell Dennis I said to comp you a beer.'

'Comp me?' she said carefully.

'Yeah. I'll join you in a minute.'

She set her book down on the desk and stood. 'This is real odd, Charlie.' She walked out and he heard her delighted squeal through the closed door. '*Cul*ligan!'

He moved to the safe, picked out the combination and extracted a small brown envelope containing a single black and white 35-millimeter negative strip. He held the strip up to the light. The first three images were party pictures of no particular value or interest, but the fourth was a real gem: a City Commissioner drunkenly sodomizing a very disinterested-looking Cupcake, her eyes locked directly onto the camera's lens.

He felt a tiny swell of regret about handing the negative over to Renata, since the Commissioner had been a law school classmate and Charlie had once considered him a friend. Bill Gerard would have used it one day anyway, he reasoned, and he pulled out his flask and took a long pull. He wondered if he should tell Vic about it, then decided there was no point. By the time he saw Vic it would be in Renata's hands.

27

CHAPTER FOUR

Charlie felt queasy as he stepped out of the office, his sinuses blocked and his eyes itchy. He pushed through the door into the men's room, stationed himself before the lone urinal, opened his fly and let flow a copious stream of urine. He and Vic had once looked at putting in extra urinals and a second stall, but they had decided it was too expensive, coming as it would from funds they could otherwise skim. Besides, Dennis pointed out, another stall would have increased certain customers' natural inclinations to lock themselves in and masturbate by reducing the peer pressure from other customers who actually needed to urinate or defecate.

This is the last piss I'll take here, Charlie thought, looking at the condom dispenser mounted above the porcelain. A cartoon woman with a salacious grin and a psychedelic dress offered latex novelties for fifty cents, ribbed for her pleasure and sold for prevention of disease only. He shook himself off and washed his hands.

A very small, bug-eyed, fortyish character in a robin's egg blue leisure suit and Prince Valiant haircut had joined Culligan at Francie's altar. Cupcake was seated at the bar reading her Gandhi book as Dennis leaned his elbow on the back bar, flipping through a tattered bondage magazine he'd found the day before in the stall in the men's room. He dangled it from his fingertips as though handling a possibly rabid bat, careful not to brush his fingers against any unidentified smudges. Charlie hopped onto the stool next to Cupcake's and gestured at her book. 'So, what's the word on old Mohandâs K.?'

Cupcake didn't look up. 'Dead.'

Dennis set a beer down in front of him and gestured at Cupcake's half-empty bottle. 'I put hers on your tab.'

Now she looked up, aggravated. 'I already told you, he said it's a comp!'

'I heard you. Charlie . . .'

'Yeah, it's a comp. I can comp the dancers a lousy High Life once in a goddamn blue moon if I feel like it.' Charlie scanned the room, starting to feel hot and prickly. He needed to get out into the cold air, sober up a little before he headed back to the Sweet Cage.

'All right, Charlie. You're the boss. I wouldn't want Vic to find out about this, though.'

'He won't unless you tell him.'

'How come Vic's not here tonight, anyway?' Cupcake said.

'Gave himself Christmas Eve off.' Charlie was aware of a slight slowing of his voice, a running together of words, a sure sign it was time to go outside and try to catch his second wind.

'What the fuck does he need Christmas Eve off for? He lives alone. Doesn't speak to Bonnie any more, doesn't see the kids ever, doesn't have any friends I know of, except the two of you.'

'I think he flew to Cincinnati to see his mom,' Charlie improvized. He pronounced it 'Sins Naddy'. It was time to go.

'No he didn't, I saw him this afternoon,' Dennis said. 'Stopped in and dropped off some paperwork.'

The front door opened and the college boys from the Sweet Cage walked in, minus the belligerent Ronny. They stopped cold at the sight of Culligan, who was staring open-mouthed up at Francie's rotating mons veneris. Cupcake rose and moved toward the boys. Charlie felt unbearably hot now.

'Shouldn't you turn down the heat a little, Dennis?'

'Sure. I bet the nude members of our staff would greatly appreciate that.'

'I see your point,' Charlie said, then stood, swigging down his beer. 'I better get going.'

He moved for the door, past Culligan. Someone would give the old man a ride home at the end of the night.

He stood there for a moment in the open door. An eight-feet-high wall of concrete blocks stood between it and the parking lot, blocking the view from outside, and the arctic wind whipped around it and under Charlie's open overcoat, peppering his face with tiny sharp snowflakes.

'Shut the fucking door, Charlie, I'm *naked* up here,' Cupcake yelled, and turning slowly he saw that she was indeed already naked and onstage, the three college boys seated obediently around the table.

'Go on, boys, give ol' Cupcake a tip, she puts on a hell

of a show,' he heard as the door shut behind him. Charlie was certain Culligan didn't recognize them.

*

I need to get some food in me, Charlie thought as the Lincoln glided south back into town, the snow coming down heavy and slick. Half the bastards in this town don't know how to drive on snow. He stepped gently on the brake, tapping it, feeling the car lift each time his foot came up, and he closed his eyes as the Lincoln went into a spin, a full 360 degrees, ending up pointed directly south again when the wheels regained their grip on the road as if by divine providence, with not another driver in sight. He regained control and a chorus of dogs started barking 'Jingle Bells' over the AM. He felt good.

Less than half a mile inside the city limits he spotted the dull orange and brown of a Hardee's sign. He swung into the deserted parking lot, got out of the Lincoln and gave the front door a hard yank. It didn't budge and he had to desperately grab for the handle with both hands to keep from losing his balance on the icy concrete. There was a professionally printed sign inside the door:

TO OUR VALUED CUSTOMERS
WE WILL BE CLOSING AT FIVE PM ON CHRISTMAS EVE
AND CLOSED ALL DAY CHRISTMAS DAY
SO THAT OUR EMPLOYEES MAY SPEND
THE HOLIDAY WITH THEIR FAMILIES

'What you got your goddamn sign lit up for, then?' Charlie shouted, kicking at the door. The interior of the restaurant was fully illuminated. He felt like throwing a brick through the plate glass. He turned on his heel and on his first step away from the door felt his left foot sliding along the slick concrete step, then his right, and then his tailbone making solid contact with the frozen sidewalk. He sat there for a moment in disbelief, his ass numb with cold and shock, his head feeling like a ten-pound brick of solid snot, fighting involuntary tears of humiliation and rage. A little green Japanese sedan pulled into the lot and stopped ten feet away from Charlie. A black kid, about fifteen, rolled his window down.

'Hey, you okay?' he said.

Charlie swallowed. 'I'm fine. Just slipped and fell.'

'Come on, let's go,' said the driver. 'He's fine.'

'You sure you're okay?'

'I'm fine, goddamnit.' He maneuvered his feet back behind him, trying to figure out the best way to get back up.

'Merry Christmas,' the kid said, rolling his window back up. The car chugged back onto the street and disappeared into the blowing snow.

He was limping when he made it back to the car. Where was he going to find food at this hour on Christmas Eve? Even the supermarkets were closed.

*

Sailing down the deserted main artery downtown, listening to the police reporter embellish his Westside tavern disturbance story, Charlie saw lights on in the window of the Brass Candle. He pulled across the empty oncoming lane and slid ten feet to a stop facing the wrong direction precisely before the picture window in front. Through the pine boughs framing it he saw a waitress bringing food to a table full of revelers within. He considered momentarily whether or not to try to turn the Lincoln around or even put it in the parking lot, but in a few minutes the car would be completely blanketed in snow and who'd know which direction it was facing? It seemed like a complicated maneuver, and he had to get food inside him immediately. The parking lot looked full, anyway.

*

He stepped into the dim yellowish light of the oak-paneled entryway, its walls draped with pine roping and thick red velvet ribbons trimmed with bells and golden cherubs stamped out of foil, the 'Hallelujah' chorus playing over the laughter and shouting coming from the dining room and bar. It felt so much more like New Year's Eve than Christmas Eve that Charlie had the fleeting sensation that he'd blacked out and spent an extra and possibly fatal week in town.

'Hi, Charlie, Merry Christmas,' the hostess said. She was a plump, pretty woman with short black hair whose name, Charlie thought, started with C or K, Christine or Kathleen or Cassandra. 'Just going to sit at the bar?'

He almost said yes out of habit, then remembered his mission. 'Kitchen still open?'

'Sure. You want a menu?' She handed him one. 'Table by the front window just opened up.'

'Great.' Charlie went through into the small front dining room. As promised, there was an empty table by the window. A tall, pale yellow taper burned in the center of a small arrangement of fir and mistletoe at the edge of the table where it met the frosted glass. He sat and looked around him and, seeing no one he knew at the other tables, stared out the window, ignoring his menu. Everything was orange in the light of the streetlamps, even the blowing snow. Things used to look bluish green under the old streetlights, before they brought in these new mercury vapor things. Or were the old ones mercury vapor and these something else? The revival theatre across the street was showing *Miracle on 34th Street*. A few customers stood in line in the lobby, waiting to buy tickets. Now and then a car passed, slowly. One came fishtailing wildly down the street and Charlie watched helplessly as it neared the Lincoln, its ass end swishing wildly right, then left, then right again. But it missed and continued on its way westward, past the Lincoln and on toward some other poor bastard's pride and joy. He wondered why he was still worrying about the car. After tomorrow it would be Deacon's. Merry Christmas, you little fuck.

CHAPTER FIVE

It was past eight. He'd been there for more than an hour now, sitting by himself, working on a plate of prime rib and a bottle of red wine and watching the snow fly outside. He still had almost seven hours to go before the meeting with Vic, and no idea what to do or where to go once he'd given Renata the negative. It was too early to go home.

'Charlie?' a voice asked at his side. His reverie broken, he turned from the window and squinted upward at a very tall, very obese man in a nicely tailored suit. 'Peter van Heuten's your brother-in-law, isn't he?'

'Uh-huh. Used to be, anyway.'

'I was wondering if you could give him a ride home. I'd hate to see him trying to drive home in the state he's in. Particularly on Christmas Eve.'

'Where is he?'

'He's at the bar. Maybe you'd care to join him . . .'

'Okay.' He'd finished his prime rib, anyway. He felt great now, ready to tame lions. Tricking Pete into a ride home would be a breeze.

'Thanks a lot, Charlie. Your bottle's taken care of, by the way. Merry Christmas.'

They love me here. I'm practically a celebrity. How can I leave? He stood and winced at the nearly-forgotten pain in his hip and limped back toward the bar.

*

The bar was jammed. Amongst the throng Charlie recognized a County Commissioner he had paid off copiously over the last six or seven years, a married local news anchor, and the conductor of the local symphony. Like everyone else in the room they were trying desperately to get laid; Christmas just wouldn't be Christmas without fucking somebody you'd just met.

Standing unsteadily against the bar, Pete van Heuten cackled maniacally at the sight of him. 'Charlie Arglist, come here, you no-good motherfucker.' The bar was very loud, and he was by far the loudest man in it, braying hoarse greetings across the room to strangers and friends alike. His tweed sport coat was several degrees beyond rumpled, its side pocket ripped down at the corner, his reddish-blond hair looked like it had been combed with a weed whacker, and still a certain loud, drunken kind of dignity clung to him. Despite the crush there was a distinct empty space on either side of him as he swiveled back and forth, zeroing in on anyone who innocently tried to occupy the adjacent spot. 'Chrissakes, Charlie, we used to be family! What a fucking great coincidence, running into you on Christmas Eve! What are you drinking?'

'Red wine.'

'Fuck that, Charlie, drink some Scotch. Barkeep, give

my brother-in-law some more of the same poison you been giving me.'

The young woman behind the bar made Charlie a drink and handed it to him, expressionless. She had not yet been ordered to cut Pete off, but she was dying to.

'Look at these pathetic cocksuckers. Piña coladas and ultrasuede three-piece suits, for fuck's sake.' He gestured at a stylish young attorney Charlie knew by sight, huddled in deep conversation with a female of his kind. 'The civilization is on an irreversible downward slide when a guy can get his ashes hauled dressed like that.'

'What you been up to, Pete?'

'Just drawing buildings. Making a fucking mint. I'm serious. I am making a fucking mint. How you doing?'

'About like always.'

'Still a mobster?' Pete yelled, and Charlie winced. 'Aw, shit, man, you know perfectly well I'm yanking your fucking chain.'

'How are the kids?' Charlie asked.

Pete was stumped for a moment. 'Ah, great, I think. Lessee, Melissa's in swim club, or maybe that's Spencer...'

'Not my kids, I'm talking about your kids.'

'Oh, my kids. Uh, they're fine. You know, pretty much.'

'Where's Betsy tonight?'

'Her folks' house, man, it's Christmas Eve. Oh, my goodness gracious...' He looked at his watch in mock horror. 'I'm three hours late...' He laughed until his knees bent under him, and he slid his back down the front of the bar until he was leaning back against it in a full crouch, wheezing, clutching his belly with his right hand, tears rolling down his face, rocking with silent mirth. The owner appeared behind the bar and, eyes on Charlie, pointed at Pete and then at the front door. Charlie sensed that Pete wouldn't be all that receptive to the suggestion that Charlie take him home or, worse, to his in-laws' house.

'Listen, Pete, I gotta go over to the Sweet Cage, you want to come along?'

Pete looked up, still laughing. 'Check out some puss? Oh yeah!' Charlie pulled him to his feet.

*

The Lincoln had a drift on the hood as deep as a mattress, and the snow was coming down quietly, slow and thick. Pete was playing with the heater controls on the dash, trying to turn it up higher. 'Christ, I wish I had the balls to do what you did,' he said, considerably less animated away from the crowd and the noise of the restaurant.

'What's that?'

'Get out of that fucking family.'

'It wasn't my idea.'

'Well, Betsy isn't about to let me out without a royal reaming. Wants to be a fucking society matron.'

'Yeah, Sarabeth was the same way.'

'Sarabeth, now there's a scary woman. Scarier than Betsy. Not as scary as their mother.'

'Formidable women, all three,' Charlie said.

Pete snorted. 'That's for fucking sure. I bet ol' Ma Henneston really thought she'd scored a coup when her girls snagged the likes of us, a lawyer and a fucking architect.'

'We're a couple of real catches, all right.'

'Christ, I haven't had a piece of Betsy in six months. Last couple of years she gets this lie-back-and-do-it-for-America look on her face, acts like I'm some kind of sex maniac 'cause I want to keep screwing her even though we already got our biblical allotment of three kids.'

'You have three now?'

Pete frowned for a second, calculating. 'Yeah. Third one's a girl, three and a half. You been out of the family a long time, Charlie.' He stretched, yawning. 'So what's going on at the Sweet Cage? That one of yours?'

'No. I just gotta go talk to the owner about something.'

'All right! Mafia business! What is it, some kind of coke deal?'

'Watch your mouth, okay?'

'Hey, did Vic Cavanaugh really slice some guy's hand off?'

'Where'd you hear that?'

Pete took this as an affirmative. 'I knew it!'

'Where'd you hear it?'

'Guy I know, this cement contractor. Told him my ex-brother-in-law was Vic Cavanaugh's right-hand man, he said he heard some guy'd stuck his finger up some stripper's twat onstage at the Tease-O-Rama, and Vic took the poor fucker out back of the club and cut off both his hands.'

'Oh, sure, that's true.' If that had in fact been the punishment for that particular offense, it would have been administered four or five times a week and the city would be full of men wearing hooks.

'That girl who disappeared, she worked for you, didn't she?'

'Not for me personally, but yeah, she danced at the Tease-O-Rama.'

'So you knew her, right?'

'Yeah, I knew her,' he said. 'Barely.'

'Well, what do you think happened? Think somebody killed her?'

'Probably took off with some guy. It happens sometimes.'

'Paper said she left a couple of kids behind.'

'Uh-huh. So?'

'So you think she was the kind of woman who'd abandon her kids like that?'

'How should I know? Jesus.'

'Paper sure made it sound like she was dead.'

'Yeah, and it also made her out to be a goddamn nun. Shit. I came in one afternoon, about a month after Desiray split, and here's this woman sitting on a barstool talking to the bartender. I thought she was applying for a job, turns out she's interviewing him for the fucking newspaper. I threw her ass right back onto the pavement, but she'd already talked to Francie and Cupcake.'

Pete laughed. 'Francie and Cupcake. Sounds like a couple of poodles.'

'Anyway, Cupcake got it into this sob sister's head that Desiray must be dead 'cause why else would she have left her kids like that?'

'Well, why would she?'

'Women leave their kids sometimes. That reporter made her sound like Judge Crater and Eleanor goddamn Roosevelt rolled into one.' The articles in the paper had caused Charlie a lot of grief, with the cops and with the county and with Vic. The woman hadn't made the Tease-O-Rama sound like a very wholesome environment for a young mother of two to be working in.

'Hey, Charlie, you ever get to top any of those strippers?'

'Once in a while, if I'm desperately horny or completely shitfaced or just generally have my head up my ass.'

'I'm all three of those most of the time. Hey, speaking of coke, you're not holding, are you?'

'No,' he said. 'And watch that kind of talk, you're going to get us both in trouble.'

*

The Sweet Cage was empty except for Sidney, who was screaming at someone on the phone when they walked in. Without looking up or interrupting his screaming he opened two beers and set them down on the bar. His face was bright red and spit was flying.

'Well if this ain't the ratfuck of the century I don't know what is! As far as I'm concerned you can grease up that Yule log of yours and ram it up your shithole!'

Charlie discreetly wiped a tiny fleck of spit from his cheek. Pete leaned over to whisper into Charlie's ear.

'If this is who you got business with, maybe you oughtta wait for a better time.'

Charlie pulled out the flask and took a swig, and took a pull of his beer. He handed the flask to Pete, who drank with one wary eye trained on Sidney.

'You'll rue the day you decided you could pull this kind of shit on me, you toothless old whore. I promise you will regret the day you were fucking born.' He slammed the receiver down, then picked it back up and screamed into it at the top of his lungs, then slammed it down into its cradle again and again until finally, breathing hard, he looked up at Charlie and Pete. 'Sorry. That was my mom, she wants me to pick up my kids tonight instead of tomorrow, she and her shitbag husband decided they wanna head for the Garden of the fucking Gods at six AM on Christmas morning.' He shook his head as if to clear it.

'Renata around? I got something for her,' Charlie said. He had the envelope in his hand. Holding it made him uncomfortable, almost as though he expected it to jump out of his hand and scurry away across the floor.

'She'll be back about midnight. You could leave it with me.'

'I better give it to her in person.'

Sidney shrugged. 'Okay.'

'Where are the dancers?' Pete whined.

'Where are the customers?' Sidney whined back. 'Rusti took off with that kid who tried to paste Culligan. Amy Sue's sitting in the office waiting for some paying customers to show. Anita's supposed to be here but she hasn't shown up yet. Christ, I wish Renata'd let me close the place up. You shut the Tease-O-Rama?'

'No, it's open.'

'Ah, maybe things'll pick up after the late-night church services let out.'

'Probably will,' Charlie said, slugging down the beer. 'What do we owe you here?'

'You're still drinking on Renata. I'll tell her you came by.'

'I'll be back by midnight.'

'Christ, I may already be gone to pick up my kids. If Renata has to tend bar tonight she will not be in a good mood.'

'She will be when she sees what I got for her,' Charlie said, slapping the envelope against his hand as he and Pete left.

Charlie put the envelope into the glove compartment. 'Where to now?'

CHAPTER SIX

The Snifter Club was nestled in the corner of an L-shaped strip mall, between a dry cleaner's and a greeting-card store. It was open from four in the afternoon until two in the morning 365 days a year. There were dim lights hidden from direct view along its red velvet-flocked walls and behind the bar, but most of the feeble light came from small candles set in round, red pebbled-glass holders on the tables. The menu was expensive and conservative: steak, lobster, pan-fried trout. Charlie had been a member since he was old enough to drink; during his marriage the Snifter had been his second home, particularly toward the end of it, by which time it had also become his primary source of sex. Half a dozen or so more or less attractive, more or less alcoholic women took him on afternoons in approximately biweekly rotation. It had been a good time until one of the women called him aside at the bar and announced to him in a grave and excited tone that her husband had hired a detective and purchased a revolver. Charlie assumed this was melodramatic bullshit, but it unnerved him enough to stop him seeing her and to change his drinking patterns. He didn't stop coming in altogether, but the divorce brought with it new habits and an urge to expand his social horizons, and for the last few years he'd been coming in once or twice a week at the most. Tonight there were a half-dozen tables occupied, and only one waiter working the floor.

Pete had hit another talkative stage, although his tone was considerably lower now. 'I figure it's what, about nine-fifteen, they're just getting done unwrapping presents, they'll start eating about nine-thirty. I'll show up around dessert and pick a fight.'

'Sounds delightful,' Charlie said. 'I can't imagine why Betsy cut you off.'

'You should come in, too. Man, it would fucking ruin Sarabeth's Christmas. That alone oughta make it worth your while. Plus you'll get to see her new husband. He doesn't like you at all. And when's the last time you saw your kids?'

'Not too long.' In fact it had been several months. As his departure date approached his usual negligence had evolved into full-fledged, deliberate avoidance, ostensibly to make it easier on the kids. He had no plans to see them before leaving town.

'We'll sit here for a few minutes and you think about it. Maybe a little more sauce'll get you into the Christmas spirit.'

'Maybe,' Charlie said. He felt bad about not seeing the kids, but he couldn't imagine any way to face them. He suspected that once he was gone the kids wouldn't care much anyway.

'Could I get another one of these, Kelly?'

'Me, too,' Pete said, draining his half-full highball glass. Kelly, a tall young woman with a black ponytail and eyes so close together they looked slightly crossed, smiled and took both glasses. 'You gentlemen are drinking with Trina tonight.'

Charlie spun on his barstool, squinting in the candle-light. Sitting at a table by herself was the very woman whose husband had supposedly hired the detective and bought the revolver. She raised her glass and nodded almost imperceptibly at Charlie, just a trace of a smile crossing her face. He got down from the stool and limped across the dining room to her table.

'Trina. Nice to see you.'

'Merry Christmas, Charlie. You're gimpy tonight.'

'It's my war wound. Chateau Thierry.'

'I didn't realize you went to Korea,' she said without much interest. She was in her late forties, Charlie guessed, a good-looking woman who worked hard to keep herself that way, then spent lots of time in the sun and drinking heavily. Her ears, throat and arms were weighed down with gold, silver and turquoise, and a few strands of her hair, frosted blonde and pulled back into a tight knot behind her head, had started to stray loose, drooping along the sides of her temples.

'Where's that pretty little nurse you're always with?'

'Respiratory therapist. I don't see her any more. Where are all your friends tonight?' He made no move to sit.

'They all crapped out on me, one by one. Everybody thinks they have to see their goddamn families at Christmas.'

'Not me.'

'Not me either. Alex and his skibunny whore took the kids to Vail. I said fine, that means I can get laid on Christmas. What are you up to tonight, Charlie? Who's your interesting looking friend?' Pete was moving toward the table with their fresh drinks.

'Sarabeth's sister's husband. Pete.'

'Hanging around with your ex's family on Christmas. That's kind of ... poignant, Charlie.' She gave a dry little croak of a laugh. 'Hi, Pete.'

'Hi, Trina. Wasn't sure if you remembered me.' He sat down, hanging his free arm down over the back of the chair.

'Sure I do. Refresh my memory, though.'

'About two years ago at the Brass Candle. You were mad at your husband.'

This stirred something. Trina leaned forward to get a good look at Pete, trying to attach his face to a memory.

'He had his hand on some little slut's ass? And I left with you while he wasn't looking?'

'That's it.'

'Christ, he was mad. All our friends were there. Everybody from his firm, everybody we fucking knew ... That was you?'

'We were necking at the bar, as I recall.' Except for a mild slur, very slight next to Trina's, Pete sounded almost completely sober now. 'Had my hand all the way up your dress and into your panties. You were pushing into it hard. The whole goddamn bar was watching.'

'Except Alex,' she said. There was new color in her

face and a slightly strangled quality to her voice. 'I was pretty drunk.'

'We went over to the downtown Holiday Inn and you called and left a message for your husband on his brand new answering machine while I was doing you from behind.'

She was genuinely flushed now. Charlie couldn't tell if it was anger or arousal. 'That was you?'

'That was me all right.' Pete was beaming.

Trina motioned for Kelly to come over. 'Kelly, Pete and I have something to discuss outside. Will you give Charlie whatever he wants on my tab till we get back?' She was already out of her chair and yanking Pete out of his by the hand. She pulled him to the front door, surprisingly steady on her high heels given how drunk she seemed. She looked good from behind, Charlie thought. Pete looked back and grinned. Charlie felt the urge again and headed back to the men's room.

It was a few rungs up the hygiene ladder from the Tease-O-Rama men's room, and instead of a rubber novelty machine, a framed girlie calendar from the 1940s hung over each of the three urinals. The soap in the dispensers was liquid, not grit, and the water was hot. He dried his hands as best he could under the warm air dispensed from the dryer vent and headed back to collect his drink.

*

'I think she's sad.' Charlie sat at the bar, bored, listening to Kelly psychoanalyze Trina. 'I mean, she's a good-looking woman, she's got money, why does she want to hang around a place like this all the time?'

'No place else to go,' Charlie offered.

'I just think she ought to join a club or something to keep her occupied.'

'This is a club right here, honey.'

'Don't call me honey, Charlie. I mean a club like a garden club or a stamp club.'

'Yeah, I can see Trina getting heavily into stamp collecting, that'd be a real satisfying substitute for boozing and promiscuity.'

'I was just using that as an example!' Kelly was in her early twenties, and she had an unswerving faith in human potential. 'If she'd just take some interest in something I think she'd get more out of life.'

The front door opened and Trina walked back in, Pete pressed close to her side. Her makeup was immaculate. Pete looked ready to drop into blissful sleep. They had been gone about fifteen minutes.

Pete sat next to Charlie and they both watched Trina saunter back to the ladies' room. 'I am definitely going to be coming back here.' The slur was back, stronger than before. 'I didn't think I was gonna be able to get it up at this stage. Christ, I've been drunk since three this afternoon. Must be a Christmas miracle.'

Kelly looked at Pete with compassionate disapproval. Here was another soul to be reached. 'I hope you will come back, Pete.'

He eyed her appraisingly. 'I will. Definitely. Um, Charlie, I think I'm about to start hitting a big fade here. We should head for the in-laws.'

'I'll wait for you in the car while you say goodbye to Trina.'

*

Pete came out five minutes later and got into the Lincoln.

'I thought that was Andy Sandoval who left with her that night she called and left the message on Alex's answering machine,' Charlie said as he pulled out of the space.

'Yeah, it was. But he told me he'd seen her four or five times since and she didn't seem to remember it was him.'

'That's a hell of a thing to forget.'

'Yeah, isn't it? She just seemed so drunk and horny I thought I'd take a shot in the dark. This is the life, Charlie, going over to the in-laws for Christmas dinner with that good Trina smell all over old Dingus.'

'Maybe we should stop somewhere so you can wash your dick.'

'No. Not a chance.' He grabbed his shirt and held it to his face, taking in a long, loud breath through his nose. 'Stinky cologne, too. You gotta come in with me, Charlie. This'll be a holiday memory you'll treasure forever.'

'You sure are animated for someone who was about to hit the fade a second ago.'

'Oh, yeah,' Pete said, 'look what she gave me while you were out here.' He produced a tiny square of aluminum foil. 'We did a couple lines in the ladies' room and she gave me this as a little Christmas present. You want to do a line?'

'Not while I'm at the wheel, no.'

'All right. We'll wait and offer some to Dorrie. She could probably use a little lift.'

Charlie turned to the right out of the parking lot heading south, in the direction of his former in-laws' house. If I leave town without seeing the kids one last time I'll probably regret it, he thought. I'll make it quick.

CHAPTER SEVEN

'How long's it been since you laid eyes on the old hell-kite?' Pete asked.

'Two years ago exactly. Christmas Eve. I was out at the mall buying all my presents at once and I spotted her carrying a bunch of bags. She pretended not to see me, so I went up and said hi, offered to help with her bags.'

'She must've hated you for that.'

'She gave me that smile, you know, like this–' Charlie gritted his teeth, drawing the skin taut on his face and extending the tendons in his throat. 'And she said, "Thank you very much, Charlie, I'll manage."'

Pete took a long drink from Charlie's flask. 'This's almost empty. We can fill it up at the in-laws'. Get some of the good stuff in here.'

They were headed down an old residential street lined with solid old houses and tall, naked shade trees. Most of the houses had strings of big, conical multicolored bulbs running along their eaves and in the trees. Charlie slowed when he saw a house with tiny points of white light draped around its frame. As he pulled over toward the curb he overshot his mark and hit it with a solid jolt, lurching upward and halfway onto someone's snowy lawn.

'Fuck! Spilled. Sorry.' Pete half-heartedly wiped at his lap with the sleeve of his sport jacket. 'Wasn't much left anyway.'

'Couldn't see where the damn curb was,' Charlie said, a little embarrassed. 'All this fucking snow.'

'You want to get down off the curb or just leave it like this? It's Christmas Eve, nobody's gonna fuck with it.'

'Let's leave it like this. I don't plan to be here long anyway.'

Pete was already scraping out white lines on the cover of a brand new Rand McNally *Road Atlas*. 'You going to join me before we go in?'

He almost said no, but he was feeling a little drunk and he didn't want to slur in front of Melissa and Spencer. 'Sure.'

He regretted it at the very first snort. After the initial burn in his nose the feel of the syrupy, bitter saliva running down the back of his throat nearly made him gag, but his grogginess was already beginning to dissipate as he climbed out of the Lincoln.

*

They walked around the east side of the house toward the back because Pete wanted to sneak a look into the dining room before they went inside. Charlie looked around the familiar backyard, feeling like a ghost in the feeble orange and purple light. It was so quiet he thought he could hear the snowflakes hitting the tops of the drifts. They turned the corner onto the west side of the house, where a faint yellow light shone through the dining-room window.

'This is gonna be great,' Pete whispered, loud enough to be heard fifteen feet away where Charlie stood watching him. Pete was on tiptoes, looking in at the last of the Christmas dinner. 'They're on dessert. Nobody's talking. The kids are all pouting.'

'I should leave.'

'Too late. You're in. You can't let me go in there and tell your kids you were here and wouldn't see 'em. Come on.' He dropped down and motioned for Charlie to follow him to the front of the house.

They climbed the porch steps and Pete opened the unlocked front door. Charlie stopped to scrape most of the snow off his shoes on the mat as Pete walked in, swaggering toward the dining room, clomping his wet boots across the solid oak floor, detouring for a brief hop to track snow and mud on a pristine, cream-colored couch. 'Merry fucking Christmas!' he called out.

Charlie followed cautiously, several yards behind Pete, ready to bolt at the first sign of violence. Pete burst ahead of him into the dining room and held the door open. Charlie stood back, peering in around him from behind. The dark green wallpaper drained most of the light out of the room. Dorrie sat silently at one end of the long table opposite her husband, and scattered around the table were five sleepy, cranky grandchildren, two women in early middle age, and a single, pudgy son-in-law, the only moving element in the tableau as his fork moved frantically back and forth from his pie plate to his mouth. The table was covered with half-empty platters:

turkey, stuffing, gravy, mashed potatoes, cranberry sauce, green beans. Of the three pies in the center of the table, only one had been cut into, and no one but Sarabeth's husband had taken any.

'Hey, who died?' Pete yelled.

There was no response. Charlie shrank further behind Pete, considering a last-minute retreat. No one seemed to have noticed him yet. He caught a glimpse of Melissa, seated next to Dorrie at the far end of the overladen dinner table. Was she six now? No, seven.

'It's the silent treatment, Charlie.'

The mention of his name didn't evoke any response from the adults at the table, but Melissa leapt up onto the seat of her absurdly oversized chair, vaulted herself out of it and raced squealing around the long, solid table and past her Uncle Pete to slam full force into Charlie. He picked the little girl up and held her tight for a second, then set her down. She pressed herself into his pants' leg, crying and holding on for dear life. Now the other adults were staring at him, puzzled and angry.

'Hi, Spence,' he said to the little boy seated next to Sarabeth's husband, trying not to play favorites. 'Merry Christmas.'

The boy stared him down without a word. Pete and Betsy's kids looked at Charlie, not quite sure who he was.

'Sorry to show up unannounced. Just gave Pete here a ride, thought I'd stop in and wish you happy holidays.'

Again no one spoke. Charlie's ex-father-in-law was twisted around in his chair, staring open-mouthed at Charlie as though trying desperately to place him. Sarabeth's husband, mouth full of mincemeat, looked as though he might stand up and bludgeon Charlie with one of Dorrie's silver candlesticks, and Sarabeth herself looked away. Betsy shot alternating disgusted looks at Charlie and Pete, as though she couldn't decide which was the lower form of life. Finally Dorrie broke the silence.

'We've already eaten dinner, Charlie. Could I offer you a glass of wine?' She smiled more or less convincingly as she said it, possibly at Charlie's obvious surprise at her unaccustomed civility.

'Don't mind if I do, Dorrie, thanks.' He walked toward her end of the table, passing Sarabeth without looking directly at her.

Dorrie got up and poured him a glass of red wine and handed it to him. 'You're limping, Charlie. Did you hurt yourself?'

'Just a little tennis hip,' he said.

'I never heard of that,' Dorrie said.

He turned toward Sarabeth, who wouldn't return his gaze. She wore bangs now, and her dark brown hair fell below her shoulders for the first time since he'd known her. Her cheeks were flushed, her eyes moist. He had almost forgotten how pretty he'd always found that sad look of hers. She pushed her chair away from the table, and he was surprised to see as she stood that she was pregnant. He felt an odd twinge of nostalgia at the sight of her belly, a small but sharp pain he wouldn't have thought himself capable of. He reminded himself that he hated her.

'Sorry,' she said, pushing past Pete. Betsy looked over at Charlie, something close to a snarl on her curled lip.

Charlie had always liked her, had in fact had a crush on her at one of the low points of his marriage, and even this attention from her still gave him a tiny spark of pleasure. She started to say something, then stopped herself, got up and followed Sarabeth out of the room, stopping long enough at the door to give Pete a hard shove in the chest. 'You shitheel!' she hissed quietly. Pete grinned, but he was a long way from the fun and fireworks he'd anticipated and promised.

'How is your work coming along, Charlie?' Dorrie asked.

'Me and Tom Hagen here made a guy an offer he couldn't refuse, that's how come we're so fucking late.' Apart from a small, involuntary wince, Dorrie made no sign that she heard him.

'Work's fine,' Charlie said. Dorrie had first turned on him in the course of a seemingly innocuous disagreement over whether or not Spencer was old enough for a bicycle. A shouting match had followed regarding Charlie's decision to give up his only mildly successful law practice and go to work full time for Bill Gerard and Vic Cavanaugh. After that day he had warily avoided her company, even on major family occasions, right up until the divorce. In the interim the phenomenon of the mostly absent son-in-law seemed to have become a Henneston family tradition.

'Who's he?' bellowed the old man at the end of the table.

'You remember Charlie,' Dorrie yelled back.

'Not Charlie, *him*,' he said, pointing at Charlie.

'That's Charlie, Bert. Spence and Melissa's real father.'

The old man pointed at Sarabeth's fuming husband.
'I thought he was Charlie.'

'That's Tony. Now be quiet.'

Spencer stood up so suddenly he knocked his chair
backward and had to grip the edge of the table in order
to keep from losing his own balance. 'Tony's my dad! I
don't even know this guy!' Charlie was genuinely surprised at how big the little bastard was getting. When
had he seen him last? Surely it hadn't been more than a
couple of months. 'You didn't even send us presents this
year.' Shit, Charlie thought, he's right. How did I let that
happen?

Melissa looked up at Charlie. 'I don't like Tony,' she
chirped. She sounded insincere, but it felt good hearing
her say it.

'I think maybe it'd be better if you left now. Perhaps
you could give Peter another ride. I think Betsy and the
children will be spending the night here.'

'I don't need a ride home, you bitch,' Pete said, but he
was beaten and he knew it.

'Goodbye, Charlie.' Dorrie smiled at him and sat back
down.

'Well, thanks for the wine.' He knocked the nearly full
glass back and drained it.

Melissa tugged at his arm. 'Guess what? I was in this
play, *A Christmas Carol*, and it was about this guy Bob
Cratchit.'

'So what,' Spencer yelled across the table. 'You were
only Tiny Tim's sister, and you didn't even have any
lines.' Melissa stuck her tongue out at her brother. 'And
he didn't even come watch!' Spencer flipped Charlie the

bird and ran from the room, adding himself in passing with a solid, well-aimed belly shot to the list of family members who'd hit Pete for Christmas.

'He would've come if Mom let me send him an invitation!' Melissa yelled after him. Sarabeth's husband followed Spencer's departure with an approving, barely suppressed smirk, and Charlie was suddenly aware of his bulk. He had a lot of fat on him, but he also had big, solid, hammy hands, and Charlie had no doubt that the man could beat the living piss out of him any time he chose to. Wondering how long it would take before Tony found himself skipping Thanksgiving and Christmas, Charlie gave Melissa a little hug and left the room.

Pete was subdued as they moved through the living room to the front door. The triumphal rout he'd expected hadn't happened, and Charlie suspected that in the long run the silent treatment would prove an effective means of subduing Pete as long as he still chose, and was allowed, to be around.

As he pushed the front door open Melissa popped out of the dining room and raced to the door. 'Will you come see me this week?'

'Sure I will, honey,' Charlie said, and she turned and ran back to the table.

They crunched through the snow across the lawn toward the car. Charlie turned and looked back and thought he caught Sarabeth standing in a second-storey bedroom window looking down at him, but it might have been her sister. She pulled the curtains shut before he could be sure.

CHAPTER EIGHT

It was five minutes before Pete spoke a word.

'Dorrie is a bitch.' He said it slowly, with wonder, like a sudden revelation. 'Shit. We forgot to fill the flask.'

'You want to go home?' They were headed west, and Charlie wanted to get Pete home before he went back to the Sweet Cage with Renata's surprise.

'I'm gonna save the rest of Trina's coke for later, but I think we need to stop for one more drink. Just one more and then it'll be time to lay down my head and dream of sugarplums and jolly old elves and all that shit.' He laid his head against the side window and closed his eyes. 'I'm not sleeping. Shake me when we get someplace that's open.'

A few minutes later Charlie pulled off the access road alongside the old state highway and into the parking lot of Terwilliger's Social Clubbe and Grille. Pete stirred, coughing, and looked around. 'Where we at?'

'Terwilliger's.' Terwilliger's was located in the corner of the parking lot of a shopping mall.

'Fuck, I hate this place. Watery drinks and all those old patent medicine ads all over the walls.'

'It's Christmas Eve. We're not going to find much else that's open in this part of town.'

'Yeah,' Pete allowed. 'I still hate it.' He opened his car door.

'It's a pretty good place to get laid, actually.'

'I don't think I'm gonna get lucky twice in the same night. Even if I was able.' Pete scowled and stepped out of the car into snow that came up to the middle of his shins. There were only three other cars in the parking lot. 'You got a membership here?'

'I got a membership everywhere.'

*

The young woman behind the bar was stacking clean glasses. She didn't stop when they came in. 'I'm closing up. Sorry.'

'We just want one drink,' Charlie said.

'Each,' Pete added, in case she misunderstood and tried to serve them one to share between them.

'I'm closed,' she said. She wasn't eager to debate the point with them. She was nice enough looking, Charlie thought, one of those Midwestern college girl faces with just a little baby fat and straight auburn hair down to her shoulders. She seemed to him too young to be tending bar. In a corner a large young man was setting chairs on the tables. Around the perimeter of the restaurant the lights were out, leaving only the circular bar lit in the center of the room.

'How come the door isn't locked? It's eight minutes till eleven, by my watch,' Pete said. 'I demand a drink.'

'I already closed my register.'

'Come on, Pete, let's go.' Charlie took hold of Pete's elbow. He shook it off.

'You know my brother here's a mobster.'

'Come on, Pete,' Charlie said. 'Sorry, honey.'

She looked over at the big kid stacking chairs. Then she softened. 'Tell you what,' she said, 'if you'll drink it right up and leave, I'll give you one on the house. I just don't want to have to reopen my register.'

*

In the end she let them stay for two rounds. She and the large young man joined them for the second. They were both university students from out of town, neither of them able to go home for Christmas.

'So let me ask you something. What's the deal with all the ads?' Pete bellowed.

'What ads?'

He made a sweeping gesture around the room. 'All these old-time ads. And all the old junk on the walls. What the fuck is the point of the old bicycle up on the wall?'

'I don't know,' she said, 'I never thought about it before.'

'Me neither,' the boy said. 'Now that you mention it, it does seem kind of stupid.'

*

'I think I made an impression on those two, Charlie.'
They were standing under the awning outside the front

door as the young man locked the door behind them. 'You know, if that kid doesn't get laid tonight it's because he didn't try.'

'I don't know. She had on one of those little Jesus fish necklaces.'

'Fuck the fish necklace. Did you see the way she was swigging that margarita? Those were strong, too. I think she's about to initiate that young man back there into the Campus Crusade for Cunnilingus.' He took in a deep, frozen breath. 'That about hit the fucking spot. You know when you have that one drink that takes you to the exact perfect stage of drunkenness? That was the one. I feel like God. Let's hit it.'

He took one step off the icy sidewalk and into the parking lot and slipped. 'Fuck! Charlie, I fell.'

'You hurt?'

'I'm too drunk to get hurt.' He struggled to get back on his feet, slipping and falling repeatedly as Charlie stood watching. He finally managed to get up on his hands and knees. The car was only seven or eight feet away.

'You gonna make it?'

'Fuck yes I'm gonna make it. Don't tell anybody you saw me do this,' he said, and he crawled on all fours to the door. He pulled it open, leaned his head and shoulders in and began spewing nine hours' worth of booze and bar snacks onto the floor of the passenger side.

'For Christ's sake, Pete, do it in the snow, not in the fucking Lincoln!'

Pete stopped for a moment, looked blearily up at

Charlie, wiped his mouth with the sleeve of his coat, and then resumed puking copiously into the wheel well.

*

'Ready to go home now?' Charlie asked as they pulled out of the parking lot and back onto the access road. Pete had apologetically scooped most of his mess out of the car and onto the snow of the parking lot.

'I know my limit, Charlie. Take me home.' His voice was raw. He looked dejectedly out the side window and then back at Charlie. 'You got any cigarettes? A cigarette would make this just perfect.'

'I quit three years ago.' In fact he had two-thirds of a pack in the glove compartment, but he didn't relish the thought of cigarette smoke mingling with the Lincoln's already overpowering odor of vomit. He rolled his window down to dilute the smell.

'Aw, Charlie, close the window, it's cold,' Pete said. His eyes were shut and his arms folded across his chest.

'You'll live,' Charlie said, and lowered Pete's window a crack to get a cross draft.

*

Despite the cold wind blowing across his face Pete was in a deep sleep when they got to his house, and it took Charlie ten minutes to rouse him sufficiently to get out of the car under his own power. If the length of Pete's body hadn't been slick with puke, Charlie would have picked him up and dragged him to the door himself.

Pete sat with his legs out of the car, taking deep

breaths, getting slowly ready to make his move for the front door. 'Come on in, lemme show you the house, it's nice, Betsy's done all kindsa shit to it since you were here last. Even renovated the goddamn attic this year. I musta killed about a hundred, hundred and fifty bats up there.'

'You had bats?'

'Just about every house in the town, if you know where to look. This town's the bat capital of the Midwestern United States.'

As soon as he managed to open the door Pete shambled over to the living room couch and fell onto it, smearing its cushions with sour, half-dried vomit.

'You want me to help you to bed?' Charlie asked, but Pete was out for the night. He wandered around the room, examining the pictures on the walls, Betsy's pricey knickknacks, the expensive furniture. He wondered how much the couch Pete was ruining cost. In the corner was a Christmas tree, trimmed with tiny, quaint Victorian-looking ornaments and – Charlie had to look twice to be sure he was seeing it right – tiny candles instead of electric lights. It occurred to him that, contrary to his old fantasies and despite that sweet face, life with Betsy would actually have been more terrifying than life with Sarabeth.

In the garage was a brand new black Mercedes Benz. Either someone had picked up Betsy and the kids tonight or she and Pete had three cars, and one of them was a new Mercedes. Charlie bent down and looked in the passenger window. The keys were in the ignition. He went back into the kitchen and wrote a note:

Pete,

My car smells like bile so I'm borrowing yours. Do me a favor and DON'T clean the Lincoln out before you return it to its rightful owner. Leave it parked outside Carswell Refrigerated Storage downtown day after Christmas with the motor running and the heater on full blast.

Charlie

He had to push the front seat of the Mercedes back about a foot before he could sit properly, and the wheel was set too low. That and the lipstick-stained Kleenexes in the ashtray led him to conclude that the car was Betsy's. It was as comfortable as the Lincoln, more so even, despite being only about two-thirds as long. He gunned the engine. It sounded good. He hit the power on the radio and was amazed at its volume and clarity, even on AM.

'Fuck the Lincoln,' Charlie muttered as the garage door came up and he coasted slowly down the driveway, then felt guilty and unfaithful as soon as he saw it sitting there on the street. He put the Mercedes into park and made his way through the drifts over to the Lincoln. He opened the door and took one last look inside. The only item of even minimal value in sight was the new road atlas, which had ended up in the path of Pete's vomiting jag. He took the keys out of his coat pocket and stuck them in the ignition, and then he remembered what he was forgetting. He popped the glove compartment open, took out the envelope with the negative and slipped it into the inside pocket of his overcoat. He felt like weeping as he walked back to the Mercedes. Now it belonged to the ages.

CHAPTER NINE

He pulled into the parking lot of the Sweet Cage for the third time that evening and swung into an empty space next to a battered black TransAm. There were eight cars in the lot now, topped with varying levels of snowmass.

He glanced into the TransAm as he moved past it. Thick clouds of grey smoke chugged from the percolating exhaust pipe, the windows were fogged over on the interior and the whole thing was bobbing up and down and side to side. Christ, he thought, first Trina and Pete, now this. How could anyone screw in a car when it's this cold?

Inside, Amy Sue was onstage and down to her skimpy blue panties. Fifteen or so spectators, several of them dressed as predicted for church, stared up at her wriggling, skinny torso. Sidney was behind the bar with his overcoat on, speaking to Renata in tones too low for Charlie to pick up. It didn't look like it was going well for Sidney.

'Can I talk to you for a minute, Renata?' Charlie said.

'Just a minute,' she said. 'I'm dealing with a problem.' She turned her attention back to Sidney, whose voice in desperation had risen half an octave above its normal timbre.

'Renata, if it was anything but my kids I'd say fuck it, but I gotta go get 'em. My ex'll have my ass back in court if she hears about any of this.'

'I just don't understand why you don't tell the old bitch to go take a flying fuck at the moon.'

'I did,' Sidney said. 'She's still dead-set on the Garden of the Gods.'

'Lousy fucking grandma, if you ask me.'

'Yeah.'

'All right, go. But this counts as your next three nights off.'

'Yeah. Thanks, Renata.' Sidney moved around the bar. 'See you, Charlie.'

'Goddamn, I don't want to tend bar tonight, Charlie. Why do people have kids, anyway? Fucks up everybody's schedule, not just your own. You have a kid, don't you?'

'Two.'

'But you don't let them run your life, do you?'

'Not really. Did Sidney tell you I had something for you?'

'No, he was too busy sniveling about his kids and how he needed to get off early. What is it? A Christmas present?'

'Can we go back into the office?'

She raised an eyebrow. 'Sure.' She yelled back into the office. 'Anita! Come here and watch the bar for a minute.'

A tall, pretty young black woman in a bright green bikini came out, frowning suspiciously at Renata. She smiled when she saw Charlie. 'Hi, counselor, long time no see.' Anita's voice was so deep that until the first time he saw her nude onstage he'd suspected that she might have once been a man. 'It's my break,' she said. 'Is this gonna take long?'

'Maybe. Quit bitching, all you have to do is pull beers. Come on, Charlie, let's see what's keeping you out all night on Christmas Eve. You?'

*

'You're limping, Charlie,' Renata said.

'Army-Navy game in '62. Tore up my knee.'

'Sure you did. Sit.'

The office was tiny, but Renata made a point of moving her chair around and beside the desk instead of behind it. She motioned for Charlie to sit and did so herself, making an elaborate, casual show of crossing her long and muscular legs slowly at the knee, then rhythmically circling her dangling right foot. Beneath her hose she wore a very fine gold anklet, just below the swelling of her delicate right ankle and above the lip of her black pump, and Charlie became intensely conscious of his need to swallow, certain she could hear each dry gulp.

'I heard a funny story about you tonight, Charlie.'

'What was that?' He fought the urge to stare at her legs.

'Heard you were waiving stage rentals. Comping dancers' drinks. Not like you at all.'

He swallowed again. 'Who told you that?'

'Doesn't matter. What've you got for me?'

He reached into his overcoat and withdrew the envelope. 'Merry Christmas,' he said, handing it to her.

She tore open the envelope, took in a sharp breath and stared back at Charlie. Her jaw had gone slack, her lips just slightly parted. I finally got a rise out of you, he thought, and then she caught herself, clenching her teeth and narrowing her eyes. She held the negative by one sprocketed edge up to a floor lamp. 'Christ, there he is. You don't have a print of this, do you?'

'No, but I've seen one and it's clear as hell. See his left hand, where he's gripping her wrist? You can see his wedding band, plain as day. You can just about read the fine print on the jar of Vaseline.'

'God, right up Cupcake's ass.' She squinted. 'What'd this cost Bill?'

'Photographer got two-fifty. Cupcake was supposed to get that, but she raised holy hell when she found out he wanted to go in the back way and Bill ended up having to give her four even.'

Renata snorted. 'Come on. Like she's never taken a load up the ass before.'

'Said she'd never done it except for love.'

'Huh. Well, maybe it's true. Takes all kinds.' She took the shade off the lamp and continued to appraise the negative, squinting against the naked bulb. 'I guess my next question is what do you want in return?'

'Nothing. It's a Christmas present. Gerard isn't operating in the city limits, he doesn't need any leverage with the City Commission.'

'Come on, Charlie. Gerard's not running a fucking charity. And I don't see him or Vic here handing this to me. What's your angle?'

'No angle.'

'Horseshit.' She sat back, uncrossed her legs, leaned forward with both feet planted on the floor in front of her and her hands on her knees. She studied Charlie for a moment, then leaned back again and re-crossed her legs. The sound of nylon brushing across nylon gave him occasion to gulp again. Her legs were a quarter of a shade darker than her bare skin, and he pictured reaching out his hand and touching her knee, resting his hand on it, feeling the cool sheer nylon and the warm knee beneath. She tilted her head to one side and looked him in the eye as though she'd just noticed him sitting there. 'Either you've lost your mind or you're about to skip town.'

'No I'm not.'

'Had your hand in the till for a while, haven't you?'

'I gotta get going.' He started to stand.

'Hold on.' She rose faster than he could have and pushed him back down into his chair with one long, slender hand. 'I'm going to have to use this right away, and I mean Christmas day, but afterward I'm going to have to be able to prove to Bill Gerard that I did this in good faith. Write me a letter turning the negative over to me and saying it was Gerard told you to do it.'

Charlie was appalled. 'Put it in writing?'

'Gerard's the only one who'll ever see it. I'll be in the clear with him and you'll be long gone.' She put her hand to the side of his head. 'This is very sweet of you, Charlie.' His face burned. She opened her desk and took out a sheet of paper and a pen.

Dear Renata,
> Bill Gerard wants you to have this
> to use at your discretion.

Charlie Arglist

He was seated behind her desk with her standing close behind him, her left breast pressing into his right shoulder blade and her arm around his other shoulder. 'That's good. Short and simple,' she said quietly into his ear. Under the desk he had a half-erection, encumbered only by the fit of his trousers and a monumental exertion of will. She took the first three drafts of the letter and held a disposable lighter to them over the wastebasket as he folded the letter and put it in the envelope with the negative.

'Seems like everybody's disappearing over at the Tease-O-Rama. I wonder why that is.'

Charlie's throat constricted a little.

'You about done, Renata?' Anita opened the door and leaned in.

'Just about. Hold your horses.'

'It's time for me to go on. Amy Sue needs to change, and somebody's gonna have to tend bar.'

'Where the fuck is Rusti, anyway?'

'Sidney said she took off with some guy when it got slow.'

'Of course she did. All right, I'll be there in a second. Shit.'

Anita shrugged and backed out.

'What else you got planned for Christmas Eve, Charlie?'

'Nothing.'

'Already seen the kids?'

'Yeah.'

'I feel like I owe you something.' She smiled and moved closer.

He squirmed. 'I didn't do this because I wanted something from you,' he began.

'You seem a little nervous, Charlie. Come on, this dirty picture of yours is going to keep my dancers naked and my beer flowing for a long time to come.' She touched his cheek again, lightly scratching his ear with her long nails. 'I think that deserves a little something.' She leaned forward and touched her lips to his. 'Why don't you pass back by at two and follow me home.'

'I have to meet somebody at two.' He felt his chest getting tight. He had never heard of anyone going to Renata's place.

'Too bad. Come on out front and I'll get you another beer before you go.' He followed her out the office door, the motion of her hips like the ringing of a church bell.

*

One superfluous beer later he pushed the front door open and stepped from the dry heat of the Sweet Cage into the blowing snow outside. In the middle of the parking lot stood a circle of about half a dozen men, several of them cheering. A couple of them looking back nervously at Charlie. Rusti and Ronny leaned against the TransAm. Its motor was still rumbling, but the rocking had ceased. Rusti still wore Ronny's sheepskin coat, and Ronny had a fresh gash on his forehead to complement her shiner, his shirtail hanging out and his belt undone. Charlie moved up to the edge of the crowd.

Sidney had a skinny kid with long blond hair in a down vest and bare arms pinned face down in the dirty snow of the parking lot, his left arm yanked painfully behind his back. Sidney's face was so flushed and he was breathing so hard Charlie thought he might be on the verge of passing out. Saliva was dripping from the corner of his mouth and freezing on his face.

'Not my left hand, not my left, fuck, not my left,' the kid begged, his face wet with blood and melted snow.

A man in an orange ski parka and stocking cap turned to Charlie and grinned. 'He's breaking that dude's fingers.' A loud crack followed closely by a shriek brought the man's attention back to the central struggle. The boy's right hand lay limp and badly swollen at his side.

'Charlie!' Rusti ran splay-legged through the snow toward him. 'He's gonna kill him!'

Charlie looked back at Sidney. It seemed possible. 'What do you want me to do?' The kid let out a high-pitched wail as Sidney broke another of his fingers.

'Stop him! He'll stop if you tell him to!'

Charlie stepped forward, past the throng, and knelt down about five feet away from where Sidney was struggling to get a good solid grip on the third finger of the kid's left hand. 'Sidney, as your attorney I'm advising you to let the kid up.'

Sidney gave no indication that he'd heard, nor that he was even conscious of Charlie's presence. The kid's eyes met Charlie's briefly, then looked away in despair.

'It's assault and battery.' Getting no reaction from

Sidney, he tried to come up with what else this was. 'Grievous bodily harm. Mayhem. In front of witnesses. You could get in serious trouble for this.'

Sidney glanced up at him. 'Seventy percent,' he said, his voice ragged. He winced as he pulled the finger back, failing to produce a crack but eliciting a pitiful howl from the kid. He yanked on it again, harder, and the crack came along with another painful yelp. 'Eighty.'

'Are you going to stop after all ten fingers?'

Sidney met his eyes again. 'I am unless you think he can learn to play the guitar with his toes.'

As Sidney struggled for a good solid grip on the next finger Charlie stood and walked over to the TransAm.

The boy yelled again, to the crowd's approval. 'Can't you make him stop?' Rusti wailed.

'Just one more to go and then he'll be done. What happened, anyway?'

'Well, first we went for a ride. Ronny and me? And then we talked, and talked, about when we were in school and stuff? And Ronny had the biggest crush on me, only I didn't know it? And we only had, like, two classes together, chemistry and English, and I didn't even know who he was? But as we were driving around tonight I, like, realized what a sweet guy he was?'

'Why don't you skip that part and tell me why Sidney's breaking that young man's hands.'

'Oh. Well, we came back here so I could take my shift? Just in case it got busy again? And we were sitting here, talking some more, and one thing kind of led to another...' She reddened, and Ronny pulled her close to him.

'We're getting married,' he said. She beamed at him.

Charlie tried again. He pointed at Sidney, who was struggling to get hold of the last finger as the crowd began cheering him on. 'Rusti, why is that happening over there?'

'Well, next thing we knew Stroke yanked the door open.'

'Stroke?'

'That's his name. My boyfriend's name? My ex-boyfriend now, I guess.' She shot a look over at Ronny, who smiled a little. 'Anyway, he was trying to pull me out of the car, and screaming and cussing me and making threats, and he hit Ronny in the forehead, and that was when Sidney came out and he pulled him out of the car and dragged him over there and started breaking his fingers.'

'I would've kicked his ass myself, only I didn't have time,' Ronny said. Rusti took his arm and studied him reverently. Her attention was barely diverted by the last agonizing pop and its accompanying cry, this one as much of relief as of pain.

Sidney rose to his feet, then walked unsteadily to the TransAm. The onlookers began stepping around the prostrate, whimpering Stroke and heading for the Sweet Cage.

Sidney leaned against the car, exhausted. 'I don't ever want that guy around here again. Understand?'

'I understand,' Rusti said.

'Good,' Sidney said. He glared at Ronny and the boy looked away. 'You ever try any of that shit on her and you know what'll happen.' Ronny blanched and nodded, and Sidney gave him a friendly slap on the arm. 'Good boy.'

'Sidney, maybe we should get you out of here before the cops show up.'

'Yeah,' Sidney said, his wind gradually returning. 'I gotta get over and pick up the kids anyway. Shit, I'm getting out of shape.' He nodded in the direction of the front door. 'Rusti, you'd better get in there and take your shift. It's down to Anita and Amy Sue, and Renata's pissed.'

Ronny piped up. 'She's through dancing.' He stepped between Rusti and Sidney. Sidney stared at him in disbelief.

'It's okay, Ronny, I'll just take this one last shift.'

'Forget it,' Ronny said. 'We already decided no more dancing.'

'Look, you little shit, I just saved you getting your brains bashed in with a fucking tire iron. Rusti, if you don't want to take your shift I won't press it, but it'd be better if you did.'

'Ronny, I can't just quit in the middle of a busy shift. I swear, after tonight I'll be done with it. I'll dance alone at home for you.'

'I already told you—' he began, then stopped cold at a look from Sidney, who appeared to be taking an inventory of Ronny's breakable appendages. 'Tonight and that's it, right?'

Rusti touched Ronny's sleeve comfortingly. 'That's it. Sidney, could you un-eighty-six Ronny?'

Sidney sighed. 'You're un-eighty-sixed.'

As Rusti and Ronny walked arm in arm into the Sweet Cage a battered VW bus pulled into the lot, swerving at the last second at the sight of Stroke lying in its path and crunching into the side of a station wagon with an 'I Found It' bumper sticker. The bus backed up and pulled into a space, again nearly running over Stroke in the process. A fortyish man with a grey beard and long hair in a fringed leather jacket got out and examined first his own front end, then the considerable gash he'd cut into the station wagon, and finally Stroke. He looked up from Stroke and stared uncertainly at Sidney and Charlie.

'He was already lying there when I pulled in,' he said.

'Maybe we should move him before some poor son of a bitch does run him over,' Sidney said. 'Come on, give us a hand,' he called out to the driver.

'Did you see what happened to this guy?'

'He went after one of the dancers with a tire iron,' Sidney said, reaching under Stroke's armpits and lifting him up.

'He's in shock. Look at him.'

Stroke's face had gone pale and his eyes were unfocussed. 'My band,' he mumbled.

Over the wind Charlie thought he heard a siren. 'Come on, let's hurry up.'

'Both of you, take a leg. We'll put him in the lot next door.'

'I think we should call a doctor,' the man said.

'He's right, Sidney. Why don't you get going. We'll take care of him.'

'All right. I just hate to leave things unresolved.' He walked over to an old white Falcon and got in.

As Charlie and the man in the fringed jacket carried Stroke toward the Sweet Cage a police cruiser pulled into the lot. Sidney had been gone barely thirty seconds. The other man's eyes widened at the sight of the black and white.

'Funny seeing you twice the same night, counselor,' the first cop said.

'Sure is.' Charlie struggled again for the cop's name.

'What's the story? One of the neighbors across the street called in a fight.'

'Don't know, really. We just found this guy lying here, thought he was passed out. We were going to take him inside so he didn't freeze to death.'

The first cop got out of the car and Charlie and the other man laid their charge down. 'My band,' Stroke murmured. 'My fuckin' band . . .'

'Looks like he took a shellacking,' the cop said. Charlie looked at his nameplate. Wilmington. Tom? Tim? 'Shit, look at his hands. You didn't see what happened?'

'Nope. Maybe you should take him to the emergency room.'

'Hey, Chet, come take a look.' The cop behind the wheel got out and knelt beside his partner.

'Jesus, Ted,' the second cop said. 'Who did this to you, son?'

'My band,' Stroke whimpered.

'He's high as a fucking kite.' Chet laughed.

'Nah, he's in shock. I think maybe we better swing him on over to the emergency room.' They carried Stroke to the back seat of the cruiser and heaved him in. 'Merry Christmas, counselor,' Officer Ted shouted as they backed out of the parking lot and onto the street.

CHAPTER TEN

Charlie's condominium was several miles past the western edge of the city limits, part of a collection of mostly unoccupied, identical luxury crackerboxes, and he did nothing in it but sleep. The year before he'd put up a Christmas tree, a real one that had become a serious fire hazard by the time he took it down in March, its needles all gone orange and scattered on the carpet around the stand. He'd set it up for the kids, then never quite got around to inviting them over. His thin walls were bare, and his living-room furniture consisted in its entirety of a black Laz-E-Boy, a matching ottoman, and a small television set. He stood there in the dark and thought about turning it on and watching a few minutes of a movie, but he was afraid of falling asleep and missing his appointment with Vic. His two suitcases sat by the door. It seemed like a lot of trouble to carry them both, and he wondered once again if he could consolidate them down to one, but he didn't know how much room he'd need for the money. Better to play it safe with one of them half-empty.

On his refrigerator door was the only piece of decoration in the apartment, a crayon drawing of a clown Melissa had given him two years earlier. He opened the door and looked inside, wondering if anything in it was safe to eat, but all of his perishables appeared to have perished. Inside the door was a carton with eight eggs in it, and he tried to remember when he'd eaten the other four. He remembered making a couple of omelettes one morning after Dora had spent the night. When had he stopped seeing her, around Labor Day? Or was it even earlier than that?

He went into the bedroom and sat on the bed in the dark. He'd only brought her here once. They almost always went to her place, mainly because his was so empty. Maybe he could call her one last time, apologize, try to explain why he was leaving, maybe try to get her into the sack one last time, for old times' sake.

Again he felt the beginnings of an erection. What was going on tonight, anyway? Maybe the fact that he was leaving town was making him horny, some sociobiological need to leave part of his genetic code behind before moving on. Maybe it was the coke nullifying the usual anti-aphrodisiac effects of the alcohol. Maybe it was the unprecedented close contact with Renata and the unbelievable suggestion of a later reward. Good God, had he actually turned down a chance to fuck Renata? What a way that would have been to say goodbye to the old town.

He shook his head, resisting his overwhelming desire to lay back on the bed. This wasn't going to work; if he stayed in the apartment any longer he'd fall asleep. It would be better to head east in the direction of Vic's house. He'd stop in at the Midtown Tap and kill some time, maybe get a chance to see Tommy after all. He picked up his bags and took them outside. He started to lock the door, then thought better of it and walked away with the key still in the lock. That would give them something to think about.

*

Driving east toward town on the state highway, he felt himself getting drowsy again, and there was a dull throb at his hip. The snow was coming down in big, slow-moving flakes now, churning brightly across his high beams, and his visibility was only about twenty feet. He was keeping it just below forty, half out of caution and half out of a dim but growing awareness of his own drunkenness. Passing an offramp just short of the city limits he pulled off on an impulse and headed west onto the access road half a mile to a parking lot behind a long, low one-storey building. He misjudged his speed entering his space and crunched the front end of the Mercedes into the orange brick wall of the building. He got out and had a look. Some of the bricks were cracked, and the Mercedes bumper was scarred pretty badly. He shrugged and went inside. It was Bill Gerard's building and Betsy van Heuten's Mercedes. Who gave a shit?

A bell gave a sad, dull tinkle when he pushed on the door. It was dark inside and smelled of ammonia.

'Charlie. I was hoping you were a customer.' Behind the counter a heavyset young man with wild curly hair was bent over a film cutter. He had on a pair of torn blue bib overalls over a pair of ratty long johns. 'Did you just crash into the wall out there?'

'Yeah, that was me. How's it going, Lenny?'

'We need a new projector in booth five. The one in there now keeps chewing up film.'

Charlie winced at the thought of shelling out the cost of a new projector; it was hard getting used to the idea that these problems were no longer his. 'Can't we just fix it?' he asked out of habit.

'It's been fixed about six times already. Tonight it chewed this one up so bad I'm not sure I can save it.'

'Slow night?' he asked.

Lenny spread his arms out and swiveled them around at the empty store. 'Had one drunk come in about eight thirty, fell asleep in booth two. Otherwise it's been like this since I got here. Don't know if it's the holiday or the storm, but at least it gives me a chance to repair the movies.'

'Too bad you have to work on Christmas,' Charlie said.

'I don't care. My family's back east and I'm an atheist. Just another night as far as I'm concerned.'

'You don't celebrate Christmas at all?'

'Not really ... wait a sec, though, let me show you something. It's in the trunk of my car.'

He went outside and Charlie moved behind the counter, examining the box to the movie the young man was repairing. On its cover a blonde-haired woman grimaced in pained forbearance, eyes closed, crimson upper lip pulled excitedly back to reveal her teeth and tongue. The title was *Backdoor Housewife*, part of the

'Anal Connoisseurs' line. On the bottom of the box were reproductions of the cover art of a variety of other titles in the series: *Cornhole Teacher's Aide, Rectal Nurse, Buttlove Babysitter, Anal Pom Pom Girl, Dirt Road Debutante* – all the vicarious Super-Eight sodomy an anal connoisseur could ask for. He looked again at the photo on the box, comparing the woman's impassioned facial expression to Cupcake's look of deadpan ennui when photographed in the same situation, and decided that Cupcake probably didn't have what it took for a big career in porn.

The young man returned carrying a large cardboard box. 'I did this for a studio arts class.' He pulled out a canvas-covered object about a foot high and set it out on the counter next to the film cutter. 'Ready?' Charlie nodded, not really very interested.

He pulled the canvas off. Standing over a prostrate Santa Claus doll was a Mrs. Santa doll, naked except for a pair of black boots, her nipples and pubic hair luridly painted in and a crude whip in her hand. Beneath her the Santa doll had on a tiny white slip, and his hands were tied together. They both had cherubic, smiling faces. 'It's called *Here Comes Santa Claus.*'

'That's nice,' Charlie said.

'They sell these dolls at crafts stores. People buy 'em and make their own little Mr. and Mrs. Santa outfits for them. Anyway, they come in the package dressed in just their underwear, she has on a slip and he has on a pair of boxer shorts. So this just sort of suggested itself.'

'How do you mean, suggested itself?'

'I got the pose from one of these–' He scanned the

S&M rack and came up with a magazine called *Dominant Bitches*. He flipped through it and handed it to Charlie. There was a photo of a couple in this very position, although the dominating female and groveling male were considerably younger and fitter than Mr. and Mrs. Claus. 'I got an A on it.'

'Sounds fair to me,' Charlie said.

Lenny replaced the canvas and put the dolls back in their box, then moved back onto his stool and resumed splicing. 'So what do you think? Can we get another projector?'

Charlie winced at the thought of promising a cash outlay, even knowing he wouldn't have to make good on it himself. From the time he and Vic had started keeping the second set of books he'd become monastically frugal with all corporate expenses, and the purchase of a replacement projector, necessary though it might be, was something he would have struggled against until it became inevitable. On the other hand, why argue about it?

'Sure,' he said. It would be Deacon's problem in two days.

'Are you kidding?'

'No, why would I be kidding?'

'I don't know, but I was expecting to have to bug you about it for six months. That's great, Charlie.'

'Merry Christmas, Lenny,' he said.

*

Rolling eastward on the access road on his way to the state highway, half-listening to an AM police report about an office Christmas party that had degenerated into a drunken brawl leading to seven arrests, he felt the need to pay a farewell visit to another outpost in his Westside empire. He jammed his right foot solidly down on the brake pedal and once again found himself spinning wildly on the ice, far faster than he'd spun in the Lincoln, and for a moment he actually thought he was airborne. Even as he realized he'd completely lost control he found himself analyzing the relevant differences between the Mercedes and his trusty Lincoln. Lower center of gravity, he thought calmly as the outskirts of the city rotated around him, that's why it got away from me. There was a terrifying jolt and a deep, loud thud as the Mercedes came down off the side of the road into a ditch with its engine dead, its lights still on and the radio still offering its cautionary tale of Yuletide revelry gone too far.

He sat there shaking and silent for thirty seconds. Then he twisted the ignition key off and then on again. The engine turned over instantly, on the very first try. He slammed it into reverse, back into forward, and back again, and in less than a minute of rocking he was out of the ditch and sailing west again on the access road. This wasn't a bad car at all. He had to admit he wasn't sure if even the Lincoln would have started right up and taken him immediately out of the ditch. After he got settled again he'd have to get himself one of these.

*

A mile down the access road he saw the light of the port-a-sign, bright yellow and buried in snow past its trailer hitch:

FRI NDLYEST MASAGE IN TOWN
COPRATE RATES NEW MASUESES

Atop the concrete block building stood a cracked plastic sign with a crudely painted silhouette of a female nude and the words 'MIDAS TOUCH MASSAGE'. Three cars were parked out front, all of them under a foot of drift and without visible tracks leading to where they sat, and tracks and depressions where at least two other cars had been parked at some point in the not-too-distant past.

He stopped next to a rusted-over green Dart, switched off the ignition in the middle of 'Have Yourself a Merry Little Christmas' and got out to survey the damage the ditch had done. More dings on the front end, but as far as he could see the undercarriage wasn't leaking. He'd check the snow under it for fluid when he came out.

A thirtyish woman with short, spiky blonde hair and a great deal of faith in the corrective powers of cosmetics sat behind a desk reading a thick paperback romance. She smiled seductively at the opening door, the smile evaporating instantly but without malice at the sight of Charlie.

'Oh, it's you. For a second there I thought I was going to have to get back to work.'

'Merry Christmas, Ivy.' Her eyes were already back on her book. 'Slow night?'

'Course it's slow, it's Christmas Eve and there's a blizzard and most people have better things to do than drive all the way out of town for a twenty-dollar handjob.'

'Any customers at all?'

'A few. Mostly guys who've just been to church with

the wife and kids and want to talk dirty. Why do you suppose guys get like that?'

'I don't know.'

'Well, we had two of 'em tonight out of, like, maybe four total. Madelyn was with this guy in there, I thought he must be hurting her. He was yelling "Fucking filthy whore!" over and over so loud I could hear it out here in reception, so I checked through the mirror and there he was, standing there in his three-piece suit with his pants down around his ankles and his dick in her mouth, had her by the goddamn ears, looked like he wanted to kill her. I would've gone in except she knew I was watching and she gave me the high sign. Afterwards he tipped her fifty. Dollars. He left this on the desk on his way out.'

She handed him a cheaply printed pamphlet entitled 'Is Dancing Christian?' Beneath the bright red cursive title a couple of crudely drawn kids, a boy with a crew cut and a girl in bobby socks, jitterbugged with satanic abandon.

'I hope you assured him that dancing is strictly forbidden here. Did Madelyn leave yet?'

'Her shift doesn't end until two.'

'Give her another fifty out of petty cash. Christmas bonus. Same for yourself.'

She narrowed her right eye at him. 'Nuh-uh. You're drunk. I heard what happened down at the Tease-O-Rama tonight.'

'What'd you hear?'

'I heard you waived stage rentals on Cupcake and Francie and after you left Dennis made 'em pay it back.'

'He did what?'

'I talked to Cupcake. What she said was, Dennis said you were drunk, and Bill Gerard better not find out you were comping drinks and waiving stage rentals, and all he needed was for Deacon or Vic to walk in and find out about it and fuck up everybody's Christmas.'

'Goddamn that Dennis. When I do something I don't care whether he agrees with it, I just want it to stay done. Shit.'

'Calm down, Charlie. It's a nice gesture, I just can't accept it.'

'I'll write out a receipt and sign it. It'll be my responsibility.'

'Huh-uh.' She was back in the world of the paperback, and he might as well have been alone in the room.

'All right, here . . .' He took his wallet out of his pocket and peeled off a fifty. 'Merry Christmas. Here's another one for Madelyn.' He put two bills on the desk.

She left both bills sitting there for a second, then picked them up. 'Thanks, Charlie.'

'Who else is there?'

'Well, there's Lynette, she already went home, and Tina didn't work tonight . . .'

Charlie took two more bills out of the wallet.

'And Cupcake's usually in one night a week.'

He gave her another.

'This is a lot of money, Charlie.'

'Is that everybody?'

'I think so.'

'Good, 'cause I got less than fifty left.'

'You sure about this, Charlie?'

'I'm sure. I got plenty of money, don't worry about that.'

'You want a blow job, Charlie?'

He replaced the wallet in his hip pocket. 'I'm not doing this because I wanted a blow job.'

'I know that. I meant more like a Christmas present.'

'Thanks anyway. I gotta get going. Have a merry Christmas.'

'Oh, yeah, I'm having one already. Thanks for the bonus, though.'

Outside there was more snow on the Mercedes, but no fluid underneath it. Truly a fine car. If he had the time he'd head back to the Tease O Rama and set Dennis straight about the stage rentals, but he wanted to stop for a quick one at the Midtown Tap before he moved on to Vic's, and after that he was out of town. Maybe he'd phone Dennis from the Tap.

*

The Midtown Tap was dark and warm, the Christmas lights ringing the room had been turned on, and Andy Williams droned over the PA singing 'The Little Drummer Boy'. The bartender acknowledged Charlie with a slight wave of his hand as he served an elderly couple at the far end of the bar. There were maybe twenty people scattered around the room, none of them looking too cheerful.

'I'd like to get my hands on that goddamn drummer boy,' the bartender said when he finally made his way over to Charlie. 'I'd wring his fucking neck. Pa rumpa pump pum.'

'Not your favorite Christmas carol?'

'None of them are. It wouldn't be so bad if Tommy didn't make us play the same goddamn tape over and over all night. I bet I have to hear the same twenty carols two or three hundred times each between Thanksgiving and Christmas.'

'That'd dampen your Christmas spirit, I guess.'

'But none of 'em's as bad as "The Little Drummer Boy".'

Charlie nodded in agreement, then jumped at an unexpected slap on the back. Tommy stood behind him, in a dark brown jumpsuit and a wide-brimmed fedora, hands on his hips, staring at him as though his presence there were a source of great puzzlement.

'How you doing, Charlie? Is Lester bitching about the music again?'

'Damn right I am. It drives people away.'

'Yeah, yeah, and right up till Thanksgiving you were saying the same thing about Peter Frampton. Drives people away, my ass.'

'It does. They hear it all day long on the radio, in the supermarket, in the shopping mall, they come to a bar they don't want to hear that shit any more. Especially "The Little Fucking Drummer Boy".'

'Watch your mouth, Les, you're talking about the fucking Bible now.'

Les sighed. '"The Little Drummer Boy"'s not in the Bible, Tommy.'

'What the fuck do you know about what's in the Bible, you fucking atheist?'

'I know "The Little Drummer Boy" is a cartoon they

show on TV every Christmas and it was never in the Bible.'

'Shut up and get Charlie a drink and leave us alone. We gotta talk.'

Lester shrugged wearily and fixed Charlie a C.C. Waterback and went down to the far end of the bar to sulk.

'Did you get the envelope?' Charlie said.

'Yeah, luckily. What's the matter with you, leaving it with Susie?'

'She gave it to you, right?'

'Sure, and then she hassled me for forty-five minutes, wanting to know what it was. Christ, that chick's annoying. She says you used to fuck her. Is that true?' His nostrils flared slightly at the thought.

'Close to ten years ago. No shit, you should have seen her then.'

'Was she any smarter than she is now?'

'I think she had a few more brain cells on active duty.'

'So what the fuck are you giving it to me this early for? We don't have a delivery until the 30th, right?'

'I wasn't sure I was going to see you before that.'

'I fucking hate it when people start to improvize, Charlie. Makes me nervous things might change. You and Vic are still with me here, right? Gerard is still in the dark?'

'Of course he is,' Charlie said. For the time being he was, anyway.

'He'd fucking better be. So how's your Christmas? You see your kids and all that shit?'

'Yeah. Saw them earlier.'

'Good for you, good for you...' He scanned the room. 'Look at these poor pathetic assholes, nowhere else to go on Christmas Eve. You guys were open tonight, right?'

'Three hundred and sixty-five days a year, Tommy.'

'Somebody's gotta stay open. That's what I figure. Let the staff bitch all they want.'

'Shit, that reminds me, I have to make a call.'

*

The phones were next to the men's room and directly underneath a loudspeaker rumbling Jack Jones's version of 'O Little Town of Bethlehem'. Charlie signaled Lester to turn the volume down, but Lester shrugged helplessly. Apparently the issue had come up before. He put a quarter into the slot and dialed.

The phone at the Tease-O-Rama rang about twenty times before Dennis finally picked it up. 'Tease-O-Rama,' he snapped.

'Dennis, it's Charlie.'

'I can't talk right now. My hands are totally fucking full and it's your fault. I got a clubful of angry customers and nobody to dance for 'em.'

'What do you mean, nobody to dance?'

'Cupcake and Francie walked out.'

'What for?'

'No reason.'

'Bullshit, I heard you made 'em pay back the stage rentals I refunded.'

'You never should have done that, Charlie. Now look what I'm in for.'

'Don't blame me, you're the one who tried to make them pay the stage rentals back.'

'I gotta go, Charlie. The house is buying a round, just so you know. These guys are pissed.'

'I'll see if I can't find the girls and get 'em back to work.'

'What's the fucking point, we're closing in twenty minutes. You guys don't pay me enough to put up with this kind of bullshit on Christmas Eve.'

Charlie looked up at the big black clock, its fluorescent violet markings competing with the blinking ring of colored lights surrounding it. It was twenty minutes to two. He hung up the phone. It was time to head for Vic's anyway.

CHAPTER ELEVEN

Vic lived in a new two-storey house that belonged to Bill Gerard. It was at the end of a woody suburban cul-de-sac on the east side, just a few blocks from where Sarabeth and the kids lived. Most of the other houses in the neighborhood had opulent Christmas decorations, and in the early evening during Christmas season the surrounding streets were typically jammed with cars full of people driving slowly around, taking in the lit-up plastic crèches, six-feet candy canes and Santa's workshops. For holiday decor Vic, whose local notoriety had not made him a popular neighborhood figure, had contented himself with a single pine wreath with a red velvet ribbon on the front door. Charlie rapped on the door's glass and waited, then rapped again louder, then gave up and rang the bell. It was seven minutes after two, and the house was dark inside.

He went around the side of the house past the garage, noting several sets of tire tracks, all of them partly filled in with fresh snow.

He stood on the back porch and looked through the glass into the kitchen. There was no sign that the house was occupied. He knocked and waited. Had Vic cleared out on him? Charlie had both plane tickets, but with the amount of cash Vic was holding the price of an overseas plane ticket could certainly be considered an acceptable loss. He reached for the doorknob and found it unlocked.

'Vic?'

There was no answer. The house was furnished in much the same empty fashion as Charlie's condo. He flipped on the living-room light. Nothing seemed out of place. He moved to the bar and poured himself a double shot of Vic's good Scotch, which was already sitting out open on the bar, next to an ice tray full of lukewarm water. He began wandering around the house turning lights on, room by room. He checked the basement and found nothing out of the ordinary, found much the same in the laundry room and the kitchen and the downstairs bathroom. Upstairs in the master bedroom he was relieved to find Vic's suitcase, packed but open, lying on Vic's bed. 'Vic?' he called out again.

Downstairs, he opened the garage door. Vic's car was gone; probably he had thought of something he needed and didn't make it back by two. Vic wouldn't have bothered to leave a note. He went back to the living room to wait and turned on the television. The only thing on at that hour of the morning was an old pirate movie and a pre-sign-off sermonette. He watched the pirates for a few minutes, then stood up and turned it off as he felt himself beginning to drift into sleep. He couldn't afford to let himself get drowsy again, not with a two-and-a-half-hour drive ahead of him. The thought of the drive made him wonder how much gas was in the Mercedes.

*

He was down to less than a quarter of a tank. Might as well gas her up while he waited for Vic to come back. He drove through the neighborhood and out onto a main artery heading south to the state highway, where he found a Stop 'n' Rob with gas pumps out front. After a minute's investigation he managed to get the lid to the gas tank open and, after sticking the nozzle in and flipping the switch, nothing happened. He leaned into the car and honked the horn, and the attendant's voice came through over an intercom.

'Pay before you pump,' he snapped, barely intelligible through the static.

Charlie went inside and gave the man ten dollars. He was about sixty, with nicotine-yellowed white hair, and he didn't seem happy about working Christmas Eve. Neither of them said anything.

Charlie pumped eight dollars and sixty cents worth of gas and went back inside. The attendant gave him his change without comment, and as Charlie turned to go he found himself looking at the candy rack. It was four feet high and six feet wide, stocked with an amazing variety of brightly colored candy boxes, and he remembered Spencer and Melissa.

Next to the candy rack was a spinning rack with plastic bags hanging down from it containing cheap, crappy plastic toys from Taiwan. He spun the rack around, examining the cellophane bags to see if anything there might appeal to either of his kids: misshapen plastic dinosaurs and soldiers, a baby doll a quarter the size of a real one, a jump-rope with pale blue handles. He pulled the jump-rope and the doll down and looked again at the candy rack. What kind of bubble-gum cards did Spencer used to collect?

'Do you still have those Wacky Packs?'

The attendant glanced over at him. 'Bottom row, far left.'

There they were. He reached behind the open display box and grabbed an unopened one from the shelf behind it, and he put the toys and the box on the counter.

The attendant rang him up, scowling, looking out between rings at the Mercedes by the pumps. 'Total's eighteen fifty-five.'

Charlie gave him a twenty, and when the man handed his change over he thought he heard him mutter 'Big spender.'

'Excuse me?'

'Nothing. I hope your kids have a real merry Christmas with their chewing gum and their crappy plastic toys.'

'They're not for my kids. They're for my sister's kids.'

'Sure they are.'

The man looked away, not caring to pursue the matter any further, and Charlie walked out.

*

As he approached Sarabeth's house he went over in his head all the legitimate reasons Vic might have had to miss their meeting time. It wasn't as though Vic didn't make a habit out of being late. Maybe there was something wrong with Vic's car. What then? They could take Betsy's Mercedes and leave it at the airport, but if Pete van Heuten had to drive a hundred and fifty miles south to retrieve it later he'd be sure to bitch about it loud and long to anyone who'd listen, and that would eventually get back to Gerard. The Lincoln might be safer, but it was registered to the company and Gerard would be sure to know about it when the airport parking authority figured out it was abandoned and towed it. Not that he'd necessarily be able to track them down just knowing the first airport they flew out of, maybe months down the line, but why give him anything you didn't have to? Anyway, the Lincoln smelled like vomit, and it was too cold to drive without the heater on.

He pulled to where he thought the curb might be in front of Sarabeth's house, a big ranch-style with a circular driveway. A string of tiny white lights ran along the raingutter, simple and tasteful, just like at her mother's. He found himself wanting to go inside and wake them all up and try to explain to her and to the kids why they wouldn't be seeing him again, but the urge was diminished by the knowledge that his departure would have virtually no effect on the everyday course of their lives. With the possible exception of Melissa, his permanent absence would be welcomed by the entire family as the final and inevitable end result of years of partial and temporary absences.

I'm sitting in a car in front of my ex-wife's house at two-thirty on Christmas morning feeling sorry for myself, he thought. Maybe that's a sign I've had enough to drink. He got out with the engine running, stepped quietly across the driveway and left the gum, the jump-rope and the doll on the snowy welcome mat. I should've bought a Christmas card, he thought. As he turned back to the car he became aware of the need to urinate again, and he went over to a bush on the side of the house and let it rip, watching the steam rise from the melting snow that covered the bush. Having melted a large patch off of it, he zipped up and got back into the car. Slowly he pulled away from the curb and headed back to Vic's.

*

Coming up the cul-de-sac he realized he'd left all the lights on in the house. He went in through the front door and began turning them off again in more or less the same order he'd turned them on. Where the fuck was Vic, anyway? Just to make certain he checked the garage again. The car was still gone. He stood there in the cold air for a minute, trying to think what if anything was the logical next step of action. He leaned back with his palm flat on Vic's worktable and it gave slightly, sliding away from him and sending him down onto one knee. With some difficulty he rose and, looking down, he saw that there was a small puddle of blood, still liquid, on the cold cement floor under one of the worktable's legs. He took in a sharp, audible breath and he felt the skin on his face tightening. He stepped back, looking up and away from it, trying without success to imagine some innocuous reason for the presence of fresh blood on the floor of Vic's garage. Detecting the first warning flutters of vertigo, he put his palm down on the worktable to steady himself and once again looked down.

On the bench vise attached to the table directly above the small, dark red pool was more blood, smeared. Stuck to the rough edge of one of its jaws was a ragged flap of skin about half an inch in diameter, the more or less parallel folds of the middle joint of a human finger.

Charlie spun, slammed both palms to the wall and threw up. He wiped his mouth on his coat sleeve and ran out of the garage, through the kitchen and the living room to the front door, which he left hanging open as he ran across the lawn to the Mercedes. He got in, started it up and drove to the end of the cul-de-sac, hyperventilating, and came to a stop. He sat there for two minutes, then three, then five, incapable of deciding whether to turn left or right.

It was two-forty-five in the morning, and the bars were all closed. He had nowhere to go.

PART TWO

CHAPTER TWELVE

He headed north out of town with no particular destination in mind and tried without success to imagine some explanation for Vic's absence that didn't imply catastrophe. Five miles outside the city limits he pulled over impulsively at a darkened Skelly station and parked next to a pay phone. He didn't know Renata's home number, so on a hunch he tried the Sweet Cage. The other end picked up after ten rings.

'Sweet Cage.'

'Renata? It's Charlie.'

'You're in a hell of a lot of trouble, Charlie, you know that? Roy Gelles was in a little after you were. He wanted to know if you'd been around.'

'Oh.'

She snorted. '"Oh?"'

'Can I come over?'

She was silent for a moment. 'Park your car around the block.'

'I'm not driving my own car.'

'I don't give a shit whose car it is, we're closed and I

don't want any cars in the lot. Park it around the block. Where are you now?'

'Out in the county. I'll be there in twenty minutes.' Again he felt his groin warming. 'You haven't heard from Vic tonight, have you?'

'No. Roy was looking for him, too.'

'It's probably nothing.'

'If Roy came to town on Christmas Eve, it's something.'

'I guess it probably is.'

He got back into the car and onto the county road heading back into town. Deacon must have gone to the bank that afternoon to make a last-minute deposit to one of the operating accounts, found it emptied and called Bill Gerard. It would have taken Roy Gelles two and a half or three hours to drive down, so he'd likely been in town for hours, and he knew as well as anybody where to find Charlie or Vic on any given night. Maybe he had already found Vic. If he hadn't crossed paths with Charlie yet it had been blind luck on Charlie's part.

*

West of downtown he drove alongside the river, the sky bright orange again, the snow coming down big and slow. He imagined taking Spencer and Melissa sledding on the sloping bank of the river, the way his father had taken him and his brothers and sisters when he was a boy, and he told himself that if he weren't leaving he'd do just that, though it had been more than a year since the last time he'd taken the kids on any kind of outing.

He wished he could call his brother Dale and say goodbye. Dale had a small farm just outside Shattuck, and Charlie hadn't talked to him in a year, either. Apart from the occasional conversation with Dale, his oldest sister's annual Christmas letter was his only regular contact with the rest of the family, and he realized that he hadn't received one this year. He couldn't remember if he had last year, either.

In the mirror he noticed a sedan a quarter of a mile back, pacing him along the curve of the river. He stiffened and tried to remember what Roy drove. He became so intent on the car in the rearview mirror that he drove straight into the empty, oncoming lane, at which point a bar of red and blue lights atop the sedan began flashing. He panicked, hit the brake and slid smoothly all the way over to the curb, the cruiser picking up speed and pulling up close behind him with a brief whoop of its siren.

He got out his driver's license and grabbed for a clear plastic dispenser of breath mints he'd seen in the glove compartment. He shook the container and rattled a number of the tiny white mints into his mouth, crunching them down as quickly as he could. The cop walking toward him stepped over the curb and onto the snowy bank. Charlie swallowed the last of the jagged shards of mint, rolled down the window and extended his license.

'I realize I'm facing the wrong direction, officer. I slid.'

'I'll need to see your registration also.'

'Okay, but it's not really my car, it's my sister-in-law's.'

'Have you been drinking this evening, sir?'

'Just a couple glasses of wine at my in-laws' house ...'

hold on, it's in here somewhere.' He fumbled blindly through Betsy's glove compartment, looking for the registration. A Kleenex box, a set of keys, a kid's report card, and apparently no registration, without which he was screwed.

But the cop was already handing him back his license. 'I didn't know it was you, Mister Arglist. You want to be real careful on this. Underneath the snow it's a solid sheet of ice.' He was polite but decidedly cool. Charlie didn't know him, but obviously he was one of theirs, which was good because this one looked like he would have dearly loved to haul his ass down to the drunk tank.

'Thanks. I should probably be getting home.'

'That's an excellent idea.' It came out as a command rather than as an actual affirmation of the idea's excellence.

'Merry Christmas,' Charlie said as he rolled the window back up. The cop strolled back to his cruiser without acknowledging the remark.

*

He parked on a residential street around the corner from the Sweet Cage and walked over toward the parking lot. It was so quiet he could hear the bare twigs above his head rustling against one another in the light wind. The lot seemed oddly brighter now with the floodlights off, and the opaque sky cast a pale glow onto the snow like ersatz daylight. Black spatters of blood were still visible against the grey of the snow where Sidney had brought Stroke's musical career to an end, and there was not a single car in the lot. He walked up to the front door, tried the handle and found it locked. He gave the door a good solid rap with his knuckle and waited. After a minute he knocked again, louder this time. He moved around to the side door, closer to Renata's office and knocked again.

'Renata?' There was no response.

He walked to a pay phone on the street corner and dialed the number. He hung up after the twentieth ring.

*

The county road leading out to the Tease-O-Rama was slicker than before, and a stiff wind had come up, blowing sparkling clouds of old snow across it. Charlie was no longer completely confident of his ability to keep the unfamiliar car on the road, but he was close enough now to the Tease-O-Rama to walk if he cracked up. He was having some trouble judging his position exactly until he saw the partially darkened go-go girl glowing against the sky. The fact that the sign was still on at this hour bothered him less than the three Sheriff's vehicles grouped together in the parking lot, and his first instinct was to pull off onto the shoulder, turn around and drive away as fast as possible. He was already easing up on the gas when it occurred to him that the presence of the Sheriff's officers might have something to do with whatever had happened to Vic.

He parked the Mercedes at the far end of the lot and crossed it to the cinderblock windbreak, where a young Sheriff's officer in mirror shades stood scowling at him.

'Club's closed for the evening. Better get along home now, sir.'

'I represent the owners.' The surly contempt on the

officer's face ticked up a notch, and Charlie suppressed the urge to make a comment about people who wear shades at night.

'You Cavanaugh?'

'Charles Arglist. I work with Cavanaugh.'

'Uh-huh. Well, you need to get in there and speak to my commander, mister, because you had some major difficulties in there this morning.'

The officer waved him through and Charlie walked around the windblock and yanked the door open.

Dennis glared at him as he shut the door behind him. 'I quit.' His right eye was swollen shut and he held a bloody bar rag against a gash on his left cheek. An officer standing next to him, studiously writing something in a small spiral notebook, looked Charlie up and down.

'Who's this? Cavanaugh?'

'Charlie Arglist. He's Cavanaugh's errand boy. This is all his fault.' Dennis swept his arm in an arc around the club. Chairs lay smashed on the stages, the floor was covered with shattered glasses and bottles, and three more officers stood taking statements from a half-dozen patrons, several of whom looked worse off than Dennis.

'You seen Vic tonight, Dennis?'

'Who cares? Look at this fucking place.'

'Did you see him?'

'No.'

'All right, now. This interview's not over yet.' The officer turned from Dennis to Charlie. 'You, sir, are going to get your turn in just a minute.'

'My turn for what?'

'Your turn to speak your piece. Now sit down and be quiet.'

Charlie looked around and didn't see any place to sit. 'I don't have anything to say. I wasn't here.'

'Do you understand what sit down and be quiet means, sir? If so you'd better do it. Otherwise I'll have to place you under arrest with those gentlemen over there.' He gestured with his notebook toward the unhappy group leaning against the wall opposite. Three of them were handcuffed, one of them weeping remorsefully as an officer patiently took his statement.

The first officer had turned his attention back to Dennis. 'So the first bottles started getting thrown. What did you do?'

Dennis looked from side to side. 'Uh, that was when I took it upon myself to fire the twelve gauge.' He pointed at the ceiling, where one of the acoustic panels was gone altogether. Next to it dangled the pathetically shredded remnants of two more.

'Usually that quiets things down real quick,' the officer said.

'Didn't this time.'

Half the bottles behind the bar had been smashed, along with a considerable percentage of the glasses. On the bar itself was a sizeable pool of sticky blood.

Charlie looked over the officers and saw no one he recognized. He didn't think they'd let him leave without good reason, but Vic wasn't here and he had to go find him. There wouldn't be much point to trying to explain that none of this was his problem any more.

'Can I wait outside?' he asked.

The officer looked up sharply from his notetaking, thought about it and nodded. Charlie walked out the door and past the wall and the first officer. 'They didn't need me after all,' he said in passing. The officer's upper lip curled a little further, but he said nothing.

Seated at the wheel of one of the Sheriff's cruisers was a sixth officer, filling out a form of some kind, and as Charlie passed it an evilly distorted face lunged cackling at the window from the darkness of the back seat, slathered with dried blood and leering at him. It was Culligan. He seemed to be missing a front tooth, and the officer barked an unintelligible command into the back seat at him. Culligan settled down and obediently leaned back into the shadows. Charlie got back into Betsy van Heuten's Mercedes and left.

Driving away he tuned into the C&W station to see if there was any mention of the brawl, but the police reporter was long off the air and the news report, when it finally came, consisted of a disc jockey reading national news straight off the wire in a weary monotone. As he passed the city limit he turned to the easy listening station, where a disc jockey who sounded like he'd been knocking them back for a while ruminated on the meaning of the holiday. This whole goddamn thing was Dennis's fault, anyway. He never should have taken the dancers' stage rentals back.

He wasn't far from Dora's place, and on impulse he made a wide U-turn in the middle of the street and headed toward it. She lived with a roommate in the eastern half of a two-storey duplex four blocks away from the hospital. He parked in front of the house and climbed the steps onto the front porch.

The living room was dark, but in the bluish light from the streetlamp coming through the living room window he made out a small, raggedly decorated Christmas tree with a few presents scattered around it. He pressed his cheek against the cold glass of the front door and held it there for a minute, uncertain whether to press the doorbell. He stepped back and leaned against the edge of the railing, trying to think of what he'd say when she came down.

Maybe she wasn't home. He stepped carefully down the snowy steps and walked up the short gravel driveway to the garage. Standing on his toes he looked in and saw two cars, one of them Dora's old yellow Beetle. He went back to the door and stood there for a few seconds, finger poised an inch from the button. Finally he pressed it. It was three-thirty Christmas morning, and he had no idea what he'd say when she came down.

A light came on upstairs and he thought about running away. He dug around in his pants pocket for a comb and didn't find one, so he ran his hands through his hair, sticking them quickly into his coat pockets when he saw her slippered feet appear at the bottom of the stairs. She had on a robe, and she crossed the living room without turning on the light. The porch light came on, and he squinted, his hand shading his eyes, trying to get a look at her face. The door opened. It wasn't Dora.

'Charlie?' It was Lori the roommate. Her face was puffy and red.

'Sorry. Did I wake you up?'

'No, my shift just ended an hour ago. I couldn't sleep anyway.'

He forced an insincere grin. 'Waiting for Santa, right?'

'What's up, Charlie?' She wasn't smiling, but she stood aside and motioned him into the living room.

Lori shut the door and switched on a floor lamp. The room was bitterly cold, even stepping in from outdoors.

'I came by to see Dora. Is she asleep?'

'She doesn't live here any more.'

'I just saw her car in the garage.'

'I bought it from her. I have a new roommate now, from Lithuania. Come on into the dining room, I'll put the space heater on.' She shuffled toward the back of the house in fuzzy pink slippers, beckoning.

'Where'd she move to?'

'Texas, a couple of months ago. Fort Worth.' She knelt before a small, cheap space heater and clicked it on, turning the dial all the way to the top, and then she shut the dining-room door behind them.

'She didn't tell me.'

'You stopped calling her, Charlie.'

'Sorry.'

'Don't apologize to me. You want something hot to drink?'

'I could use a drink, now that you mention it.'

'All I got is coffee. I quit drinking.'

'Oh. Yeah, that'd be fine, if you're having some anyway.'

Without a reply she went into the kitchen, the door

swinging shut behind her. Charlie sat down at the round, bare table, and as the space heater's coils slowly shifted from grey to orange he took inventory of the tiny, sadly familiar dining room. On the shelf were two oversized coffee table art books he'd given Dora, and last year's Christmas gift to her – a framed pastel-toned poster of an Indian woman sitting on a blanket mashing corn – was still hanging on the wall. He'd bought it a year ago tonight, in fact, at a joyless little gift shop downtown that had gone out of business shortly afterward. Christmas morning Dora had given him the impression that she was crazy about it.

Through the kitchen door the microwave hummed, and Lori poked her head through. 'Milk? Sugar?'

'No, thanks.' Her head disappeared again and the microwave bell dinged. Ten seconds later Lori appeared with two mugs, each with a spoon.

'Might need a little more stirring. Sorry it's instant.'

She plopped down onto one of the chairs. 'Merry Christmas.'

'Yeah, Merry Christmas. You going to see your family tomorrow?'

'Mine's all in Indiana.' She sipped tentatively at the coffee, testing it for heat. 'You going to see your kids?'

'Saw them tonight. Over at the in-laws'.' He put the mug to his lips, took in a small amount of hot, corrosive liquid, and surreptitiously spat it back into the mug.

She gave him a curious look, head tilted to one side, eyes narrowed. 'You get back together with your ex?'

'No, I just went over there for a few minutes.'

'Because that's what Dora thought maybe happened.'

'No.'

She was staring straight at him, and he found it hard to meet her gaze. 'I'm sorry.'

'What for?'

'I'm sorry I hurt Dora.'

'Charlie, you're so full of yourself it's not even funny.'

'What are you talking about?'

'I don't mean to burst your bubble, Charlie, but you didn't really hurt Dora. I mean, sure, a little at first, but she got over that quick enough. She knew it wasn't going anywhere, anyway. She'd known it for a long time.'

'She did?'

Lori leaned back. 'What do you want me to tell you, Charlie, that you broke her heart? Shit, she was dating one of the interns before you even quit calling. And if he couldn't keep her from moving to Fort Worth, I certainly don't think you could've. Don't worry about it. Your conscience is clear.'

'That's a relief,' he said, though oddly it wasn't.

'I'm not trying to break your balls, honest. So how's work and stuff?'

'Same as always.'

'They ever find out what happened to that stripper who disappeared? Dora said you knew her pretty well.'

'Look, I probably should get going. Got six o'clock mass in the morning.'

Lori snorted. 'Yeah, you and me both.'

*

At the front door Charlie gave her a peck on the cheek.

'Good to see you again, Charlie. Sorry I'm feeling like such a bitch tonight. And sorry about the coffee.'

'Thanks for letting me come in. Nice to see you, too.'

'You know, you could call me sometime. It wouldn't have to get complicated.'

'Yeah, maybe I'll do that.' He opened the door and stepped back onto the porch.'

'Sure. Merry Christmas,' she said, and shut the door behind her. As he stepped off the porch a woman in a flannel robe stared at him from the front window of the other unit of the duplex, her angry eyes wide open and her face pinched tight in the soft multicolored light of a Christmas tree.

*

He got back onto the state highway headed west and pulled onto the access road leading to the Midas Touch, dark now and abandoned-looking, the only building for half a mile in either direction. He sat in the car and sorted through his key ring until he found a key marked MASS. A piece of hand-printed notebook paper was thumb-tacked to the front door:

WE WILL BE CLOSED CHISTMAS DAY
SO OUR EMPLOYEES MAY SPEND IT
WITH THEIR FAMILYS

Inside it was cold and silent, with a faint moldy smell. He turned on the light in the front room and a brightly colored plastic bas-relief of Santa's head winked knowingly at him from the cheap wood paneling.

'Anybody here?' There was no answer. He turned to leave and noticed that he'd tracked in mud and, leaning on the front desk, picked up his left foot to examine the sole. The shoe was wet, with tiny crystalline chunks of hardened snow clinging to it, but no mud to speak of. Looking back down at the mud he saw a messy trail of it leading to Encounter Room 2 and felt his sphincter snap tight. Involuntarily he glanced back at Santa, whose red-faced leer had assumed a threatening aspect, and cautiously began following the tracked mud.

The trail led to the massage table, which was muddy and smeared with still-tacky blood, then continued out to the storage room, and finally to the back door. Charlie looked at the door for a minute, wondering whether someone was outside it or not. The alarm light was on, and on the back door it could only be turned on and off from the inside. He stuck his key into the alarm box, turned it off and stepped outside, apparently still alone. Two parallel furrows in the snow led to a patch of snow flatter than any of the surrounding area, about six feet long by three feet wide. He stood over it for a minute or so, then went back inside to find a shovel and, if possible, a drink.

CHAPTER THIRTEEN

He pulled open Ivy's top drawer and found nothing but blank Mastercharge slips and a stack of special coupons: Buy five Oriental Massages and get a *free* Breast Massage. The other drawers were empty except for a couple of dense, well-thumbed paperback romances. He was sure Ivy kept a bottle in the desk; she must have taken it home with her for the holiday. He didn't feel capable of digging up whatever was out back without a fortifying drink, but after a cursory search of the drawers and cabinets in the Encounter Rooms he had to face the fact that there was not a drop of liquor to be had in the Midas Touch that Christmas morn.

A shovel leaned against the wall of the storage room. Its blade was wet with greyish brown, frozen mud. Charlie picked it up, turned on the rear floodlight, and pushed his way out the back door. The rear of the property was enclosed by an old warped chainlink fence, and beyond the fence he saw no sign of life. He stood for a moment over the spot, then began to dig. If Vic was down there, then the money was gone, Charlie was exposed and his only option was to run. He kept digging anyway, more certain with every shovelful that it was Vic. The pain in his hip, almost forgotten, began to reassert itself.

The soil turned more easily than he had expected, big chunks of solid, semi-frozen earth already broken by the earlier excavation. His heart pounded from the effort nonetheless, and by the time he hit something soft about three feet down he was wheezing desperately. He uncovered most of the thing, a canvas package tied with twine and looking very much like a human body. He looked down at it, feeling tiny beads of sweat freezing on his face. He cut the twine at the head with his penknife and then sawed through the canvas. Beneath it lay the back of a human head, its short dark hair matted with blood. It might have been Vic or it might not. He became conscious of a stitch in his side, a consequence of the unaccustomed physical exertion, but he felt strangely calm. He tried to turn the body over so he could get a good look at the face, but the canvas was stuck fast to the soil beneath it and it wouldn't budge. He took a deep, painfully cold breath, got a firm grip on the head itself with both hands and gave it a good solid twist. It didn't budge, but there was a small, encouraging crackle and he tried again, putting his shoulders into it. It gave this time with a slow, wet splintering sound punctuated by several sharp snaps. The bloody face, its eyes and mouth open in apparent surprise, was Deacon's. Standing up and appraising the whole canvas Charlie saw that the body was far too small to have been Vic. He felt giddy with joy and disbelief. For the moment, anyway, he had a reprieve.

*

He phoned Vic's house from the front room. The other end picked up, but no one spoke. He hesitated. 'Vic?'

'What the fuck's going on? I got home and the front door was wide open. I almost had a heart attack. Where are you?'

'The Midas Touch. Deacon's dead.'

'Christ, what'd you do, dig the little fucker up?'

'I saw there was a grave, I thought it was you.'

'That's real thoughtful of you, Charlie. I hope you put him back the way you found him.'

'Sure I did, what do you think?' He hadn't. In his excitement he'd raced straight back inside, leaving the grave open and the floodlight on.

'You better get over here. We got more trouble.'

'What kind of trouble?'

'I'll tell you when you get here. You've spilled enough over the phone for one night.'

*

He covered the canvas package with the frozen blocks of mud, but couldn't get them on an even plane with the rest of the ground. He tossed a few chunks aside, settling finally for what was at best a more or less even coverage, which he then layered over with snow. When he stood back it still seemed to him lumpy and uneven, and he began smashing it flat with the shovel. After eight or nine solid blows, he was wheezing again and gave it up. He shoveled some more snow onto the top, smoothed it over with the shovel and turned to go. At the door he stopped. Deacon had been a nasty little homunculus and had most likely died trying to get him killed, but it seemed wrong to leave without a prayer of some kind. He mumbled a Hail Mary, an Our Father and what he could remember of the 93rd Psalm and then he opened the back door. Fat lot of good that did Deacon, he thought. He stamped around the area bounded by the fence, breaking the crust of the snow so that the disturbed area wouldn't stand out so badly, then turned off the flood and looked out at the grave, trying to decide whether it was any more or less obvious than when he'd first seen it. He decided it looked all right and pulled the back door shut.

*

It was four-forty-five in the morning when he got to Vic's house. The lights were off again, and he went around the back way. Vic was waiting for him in the kitchen, wearing a bright blue down ski parka.

'What the fuck took you so long?' His flat, round, usually pale face was bright red, from anger or exertion or cold.

'Just straightening up at the Midas Touch.'

'No point. They'll find Deacon the 27th or 28th no matter what we do, and by then we'll be long gone. Come on downstairs, I got something to show you. You'll get a kick out of this.'

*

In the center of Vic's basement was a large footlocker riddled with bullet holes, all of them burst outward as though shots had been fired by someone inside it.

'We're gonna have some fun on our way out of town, Charlie.'

'You're a fucking dead man, Cavanaugh.' The angry voice came from inside the footlocker, which scuffled and scratched uselessly on the dust of the cracked green linoleum.

'Big talk from a guy locked inside a trunk, Roy.'

'Who's with you? Is that Arglist?'

'Shut up. Give me a hand here, Charlie, let's take him upstairs and get him into the Lincoln.'

'I don't have the Lincoln.'

'What are you driving, then?'

'A Mercedes.'

'What the fuck you driving a piece of foreign shit like that for? You got the best American car there is.'

'The Lincoln's full of puke.'

Vic gestured at the gyrating footlocker. 'Will that thing fit into the trunk of a Mercedes?'

Charlie shook his head. 'I'm not sure. Might have to put it into the back seat.'

'That's no good. I don't want to have to listen to this cocksucker all the way to Lake Bascomb.'

'Arglist, listen to me.' The voice was ragged and breathless. 'You could still get out of this alive if you help me out of here. He's gonna cut you out anyway.'

'Shut up!' Vic gave the trunk a vicious kick, then pulled back in pain. 'Jesus, my toe.'

'Why don't you just shoot him?'

'Because I want to see him sinking slowly into Lake Bascomb. Besides, we have to get rid of the body somehow.'

'So what happened, exactly?'

'I was waiting for you, and around about one o'clock

I heard a noise, so I went outside to check it out. So there's Deacon, hiding behind the side of the house. I coldcocked him and took him into the garage and got him to tell me what he knew and who else knew it.'

'You hear me, Charlie? I'm offering you a deal.'

Vic started to kick the trunk again, thought better of it and grabbed a length of steel rebar and smashed it on the lid.

'Shut up, I said! Come on, Charlie, let's go upstairs.'

They climbed the stairs, Roy Gelles's offers to cut a deal with Charlie following them hoarsely up into the kitchen.

'Come on into the living room, Charlie, I'll see if I can't salvage us a drink from the wreckage before we go.'

The living room had been demolished. Furniture was overturned, upholstery slashed, drawers yanked out. The television lay on its side, a hole the size of a cue ball in its screen. The bottles on the bar, which had been full when Charlie was there waiting for Vic, were now empty. Vic went over to the liquor cabinet and opened it, searching for a bottle of anything at all.

'This is adding insult to injury, you know? He just fucking poured it out.' Vic shook his head at the empty bottles as though examining a desecrated church.

'How'd he get into that trunk?'

'Oh, yeah. So I got back from getting rid of Deacon and there was Roy, tearing the place apart. I snuck up behind him with that chunk of rebar and coldcocked him just like I did Deacon, took his gun, pulled him downstairs and stuffed him into the trunk. He's wedged in there tight, Charlie. I was so tired I forgot to check if he had another piece on him. Turns out he did. I about had a fucking heart attack when bullets started coming out of that trunk, I'll tell you.' He rose, shaking his head sadly. 'Not a drop.'

'Any beer in the fridge?' He wanted a drink. His head was starting to hurt.

'Nope. Well, you have to drive anyway. I figure we can still make the eleven AM flight to JFK, even after a stop at Lake Bascomb. Come on, move your Mercedes into the garage and let's see if we can't fit old Roy into the trunk.'

*

Charlie was surprised to find that the footlocker was indeed too long to fit into the trunk. He had begun to believe that the car would never let him down. 'We could shove it halfway in lengthways, stick a red cloth on it and tie the lid down with twine,' Vic said.

'There are traffic laws regarding oversize loads in trunks.'

'Your problem is you think like a fucking lawyer, Charlie. Let's just do it and get this done so we can get out of town.'

'If we get it wrong, some cop might decide to stop us and tell us how to do it right. What do we do when the footlocker starts talking to him?'

'That won't happen,' Vic said, but his face was troubled. 'I see people do it like that all the time.'

'Come on, it's maybe twenty minutes to Lake Bascomb, even with snow. Let's just put him in the back seat.'

The voice rose from the locker again. 'I'll make it worth your while, Charlie. I'll say I couldn't find you. You can take the money with you. All of it. I'll bring back Vic's head in a hatbox and that'll be enough for Bill.'

'You feel like listening to that the whole way out there, Charlie?'

'We're less likely to get stopped that way. And this way we can fit all the luggage in the trunk and we won't have to repack it afterward.'

Vic sighed. 'Okay, you win. Whatever Charlie wants. I'm tired. Let's just get the bastard into the car and get going.'

They lifted the footlocker by the handles. Roy's struggling inside caused Charlie's grip to loosen, and he dropped his end hard onto the cement floor of the garage, prompting a cry of pain and surprise from within. Again he lifted his end and they maneuvered it successfully, though with some difficulty, onto the back seat. Charlie was again impressed by the car's deceptively large interior.

'You know, that's a hell of a big footlocker. I'm not sure this thing would have fit into the Lincoln's trunk, either.'

'Yeah, maybe not,' Vic said. 'Let's get the bags loaded and split.'

*

There wasn't a car in sight as they turned off the old state highway three miles east of town. Roy's pleadings had ceased and been replaced by low, garbled mumblings. Charlie found that he was almost able to block the noise out of his mind beneath the din of Christmas carols from the easy listening station, and then Vic reached out and turned the radio off. 'Heard enough of that shit to last me a lifetime,' he said, and the incoherent moaning was the only sound to be heard over the engine and the heater.

Roy probably wasn't getting much air through those bullet holes, Charlie thought. Without them he most likely would have suffocated already. Vic sat staring straight ahead, his face blank, saying nothing. He looked like he might be headed to cash in some empty pop bottles, or pick up his dry cleaning.

'I gave the negative to Renata,' Charlie said absently. He still wanted a drink.

Vic's brow creased. 'What negative?'

'Cupcake.'

Vic turned to face him, stunned. 'You gave her the negative? What the fuck for?'

He shrugged. He shouldn't have mentioned it. 'Christmas present.'

'That's not funny. You don't go doing things like that. It upsets the balance of power.'

'What do we care? We're gone anyway.'

'That's not the point.'

'So it's okay to fuck Bill Gerard over for three and a half years and then empty his operating accounts, but it's not okay to give away a lousy photograph?'

Vic shook his head, disgusted. 'Never mind. Just never mind.'

'She told me Roy was in looking for us both tonight.'

'Why would she bother to tell you that? Like it's something sinister? What did you tell her, anyway?'

'Nothing.'

'Come on, Charlie, why'd she think you were giving her the fucking negative? Of all the dumb bastards I've ever met in my whole life you're the one. You are the one.'

'Vic, Bill Gerard knows. That's why we have Roy locked in a box back there.'

Vic was very quiet. 'That's not the point,' he said softly. They were silent for a few seconds, and Charlie made out a prayer coming from the box, a series of alternating Hail Marys and Our Fathers.

Vic shook his head. 'Listen to him, trying to get in good at the last minute.'

'It's funny, I just said a Hail Mary earlier tonight for the first time in I don't know how many years, and here it is popping up again.'

'That's inspirational.'

'You Catholic, Vic?'

'Yeah, course I am. So are you, right?'

'Used to be, anyway.'

'What do you mean, used to be? Once a mackerels-napper, always a mackerelsnapper.'

'Well, I married a Congregationalist, so my kids are being raised that way.'

'I'd never let my kids get raised anything but Catholic. Not that Bonnie'd ever try.' Vic turned around and looked back at the footlocker. 'Hey, Roy, what've you done since your last confession? Nothing too bad, I hope.' He laughed. The raw monotone chant from the footlocker abruptly ceased, and Vic laughed louder. 'Sounds to me like Roy's headed straight for hell.'

'I want to talk to a priest,' Roy said. He sounded drunk.

'That's right, isn't it, Charlie? You die with anything worse than a venial on you without confessing you go directly to the hot place.'

'That's what I seem to remember, but I'd really have to ask a priest or a canon lawyer. There might be some sort of exemption if you're genuinely unable to get to a priest and you genuinely want to confess. Maybe some extra time in Purgatory.'

'Fucking lawyers, always looking for a loophole. I say Roy's going right from Lake Bascomb into the lake of fire.'

At that Roy began kicking fiercely at the top of the box, and Charlie began to imagine dropping the trunk into the frigid black lakewater. He wasn't sure he could make himself do it, wasn't even sure he could stand by and let Vic do it. Why couldn't Vic have just shot the poor bastard? This was a long way out of their way and a lot of time out of the schedule just to satisfy Vic's Grand Guignol sense of revenge. Maybe Roy was right, and once they were out at the lake Charlie would be joining him under it. Maybe he should consider accepting Roy's offer. He knew the part about letting him get away with the money was a bluff, but it seemed to him there was a good chance Roy would let him live. Not a bad quid pro quo, it seemed to Charlie. Roy bellowed incoherently inside the footlocker, probably delirious from the lack of oxygen, or maybe from the blow to the head.

'You ever killed anybody before, Charlie?' Vic looked at him sideways.

'No.'

'Thought you were in the army. Weren't you in Vietnam?'

'I was stationed in Germany. I was out before they started the big buildup over there, anyway.'

'I could've gone to Korea, if I hadn'ta been in jail. I even volunteered to go if they'd let me out, but they didn't bite. I would've gone, too. I wanted to.'

Charlie cleared his throat. 'So how come you went all the way out to the Midas Touch to bury Deacon?'

Vic shrugged as if it were obvious. 'If I left him in the house or buried him in the yard someone might've seen me, and if I ever got picked up it'd be that much easier to pin it on me. And I figured if you and me are missing, and Roy's missing, and they find Deacon's body, who're they gonna blame for all of it?'

'Bill Gerard?'

'Exactly.'

Roy's breathing was ragged now, loud heaving wheezes.

'Maybe we should let him have a little air in there, Vic.'

'Are you nuts? He'll be dead in ten minutes.'

Charlie pondered the idea of Bill Gerard going down for the whole mess. That he and Vic might be considered possible victims instead of perpetrators hadn't occurred to him before this. They would be counted as missing and presumed dead. A sudden, intrusive thought brought with it a momentary wave of panic.

'Hey, Vic?' He felt his voice rise half an octave on the second syllable.

'Yeah?' Vic was looking away from him, out the passenger side at the passing snowscape of low fences and telephone poles.

'What do you think really happened to Desiray?'

Vic said something under his voice without turning.

'What? I didn't hear what you said.'

His voice rose as he repeated himself, still facing out the window. 'I said don't worry about Desiray.'

'I'm not worried, I just, you know, I wonder sometimes.'

'Don't think about it.'

They drove on, accompanied by the loud, wet gasps from inside the footlocker. Finally Vic faced forward.

'Look, Charlie, she knew what we were up to.'

'How'd she figure it out? Nobody else did.'

'I was screwing her at the time. She was around a lot, she started putting things together. One day she just asked me, are you ripping off Bill Gerard? She caught me off guard. I told her.'

'You told her?'

'What was the point of denying it at that stage? Jesus, she'd already figured it out. She wanted to cut in, come along with us. She wanted to come with me, specifically.'

'So you killed her?'

'What would you have done? She wanted a third of it. That's one-third of my half and one-third of yours.'

'Jesus, Vic, she had two kids.'

'Hey, those kids are with her sister and brother-in-law. The sister's a nice churchgoing gal, nothing at all like Desiray. She's a much better influence on those kids than that greedy whore was. And don't forget, you're part of it. I was defending your interests just as much as my own.'

'So where's the ...' He stopped himself and rephrased it. 'Where'd you put her?'

'Same place as Roy's going. In another footlocker.'

'Jesus. You didn't put her in there alive, did you?'

'Would you feel better if I said no?'

He nodded. 'Yeah, I would.'

'Okay, then. She was dead before the box hit the water.'

Neither of them spoke again until they got to the lake.

*

There were no tracks in the snow leading to the short wooden dock. Charlie brought the car to a stop about ten feet away from it, then got out and opened the rear driver's side door. Vic opened the other door and pushed as Charlie pulled. Charlie's hip was throbbing again, and he slipped, pulling the footlocker down with him and out of the back seat. When it hit the ground a sound came from inside it like a basketball deflating. Another inch forward and its corner would have hit him right in the balls.

'You okay?'

'I'm fine,' he said, certain that Vic intended to kill him right there, the second he was no longer needed to help push Roy under the waves.

He stood up and brushed himself off, the pain in his

hip worse. They carried the footlocker toward the dock, with Vic taking the front end and walking backward. Vic stepped carefully onto the snow-covered dock, and before he'd taken two more his foot slid out from under him. The locker hit the planks hard on Vic's end, the gasp from within barely noticeable this time.

'Shit. Come on, let's get this cocksucker in the water and hit the road. Set it down and push.' Vic stood again and began dragging the locker to the end of the dock. Charlie pushed, sliding the locker over the bumpy planks.

'Okay, stop.' Vic stood at the very edge of the dock. He turned to look out at the lake, frozen over and covered with a thick layer of luminous snow. He let out a satisfied sigh. 'It sure is pretty, Charlie.'

'Yeah.' He watched Vic admiring the view, the footlocker heavy behind his knees, the dock slick with snow, and as he reached his decision he was already bending over to shove the footlocker, putting his shoulder into it. It slammed into the back of Vic's knees, and his feet flew out from under him. He managed to keep himself vertical, his feet dropping toward the ice, and his arms flew out behind him and he barely clung with one, struggling, to the end of the dock for a moment. Then he lost his hold and, after a brief, silent fall, hit the ice with a thud and a crack, but no splash. 'You dumb son of a bitch! Help me up!'

Charlie leaned over the footlocker and looked down at Vic's dark silhouette, spreadeagled on the ice to distribute his weight evenly. The drop had been a good eight feet; the lake was low this year.

'Hold on, I'll go get something for you to grab onto.'

'Hurry the fuck up.'

Charlie walked slowly back to the car and opened the trunk. He reached behind the bags and pulled out a tire iron and a two-piece jack of a type he'd never seen before, then returned to the dock.

'Hurry up, this ice ain't gonna hold forever.'

Charlie winced as he dropped the first part of the jack a few inches from Vic's face. It smashed straight down through the snow, through the ice and into the water. There was a creaking sound like an old house settling.

'What the fuck are you doing, Charlie?' Vic very carefully raised his head above the ice, inching himself away from the jack's hole and its spreading cracks, moving away from the shore in the process.

'Sorry, Vic.'

'You piece of shit.'

'You were going to kill me.'

'You don't know where the money is, Charlie. You're screwed without me.'

'It's in one of your suitcases.'

'No it's not.'

The creaking came again, louder and a little higher in pitch, and Vic moved very gingerly, looking toward the shore and reaching into his coat pocket for something. Charlie dropped the other part of the jack. It, too, went straight down, hitting less than a foot from Vic's chest and the ice opened up under him. He disappeared for a second, and then his head reappeared, sputtering. Only his head and the shoulders of his down jacket were visible above the surface as he began treading water.

'Jesus Christ, it's cold...' His voice broke, shivering. 'Charlie, help me. I wasn't gonna kill you. I swear.'

Charlie stepped off the dock and rummaged around in the snow for a rock. He returned to the dock's edge with a couple of big ones, the larger a good ten pounds, and he dropped the smaller one. He missed Vic's head, and the rock made a loud, plosive sound as it hit the water. Charlie dropped the second rock, and Vic yelled in pain and surprise as it hit the top of his head with a surprisingly wooden sound. Vic stared up at Charlie, dazed, and then he went under with an audible intake of lakewater. Charlie watched the jagged black hole for a minute and a half, timing it with his watch, then turned to open the footlocker. He worried briefly about Vic's coming up through the hole in the ice once he began to bloat, but he decided that the ice would probably reform over the hole by then. In any case it was a big lake, and he was unlikely to come up right where he went down.

'I'll have you out of there in a second, Roy, and we'll talk about a deal.' His great, life-changing plan was over now, years of careful planning and deception over and done with, and poor Desiray lay dead in a trunk just like this one in the icy water beneath him for nothing. He felt curiously relieved, prying at the cheap combination pad-lock with the tire iron until its hasp twisted and snapped open.

'Roy?' He reached inside and gave him a shake. Roy's eyelids half covered his motionless eyes and his jaw hung loose, his tongue visible between his teeth. Charlie checked his neck for a pulse and found none, but he didn't really know exactly where to press. He shook Roy harder. 'Come on.' Roy didn't move. He remembered an old story his great-grandfather Arlen used to tell about a country doctor who'd revived a supposedly dead tenant farmer by breaking his big toe. The farmer had shrieked in pain and surprise and sat up, alive and apparently healthy, prompting talk locally of resurrection and miracles, but the toe turned black with gangrene and killed him a week later. The tale was always accompanied with gleeful laughter on the part of the storyteller.

He didn't want to take off Roy's shoe, so he grabbed the clammy left hand and snapped its little finger. The expression on Roy's face didn't change. He reached down into the footlocker and came up with Roy's empty pistol, a tiny nickel-plated thing he must have kept hidden in his sock. He didn't feel right stealing from a dead man, and in any case he didn't know where to get ammunition for it or even what kind of ammunition it took, but he thought it might be good to have. He dropped it into his inside overcoat pocket. 'Sorry, Roy.'

He closed the footlocker and shoved it off the end of the dock. It instantly tore a long rectangular hole in the ice just to the left of the first. It floated for a moment, foundered, and sank.

CHAPTER FOURTEEN

Vic's suitcases contained eight or ten changes of warm weather clothes, three pairs of alligator boots, a shaving kit, and a thousand dollars in traveler's checks. There was no other money. Charlie hauled both suitcases to the dock and dropped them into the larger hole, got back into the Mercedes, turned the radio back on and started the drive back to Vic's house.

An all-string orchestra made its way through a tepid arrangement of 'White Christmas' as he drove along the blank drifts and poorly kept fences on either side of the road. The ragged-voiced disc jockey murmured in a slurred, hushed tone of awe over the end of the song about the deeper meaning of this particular snow, suggesting that it might be a Christmas miracle. Charlie thought for the first time in years of his eighth Christmas when it had snowed three days straight, the year he got the Labrador puppy on Christmas morning. Even though it was intended as a pet for all six kids, the pup had attached itself to Charlie immediately. He named him Duke, and Duke was always primarily Charlie's dog, at least until he went away to college. Whenever he came home on a break Duke was hysterical with joy, whining and barking and licking, and his eyes took on an almost comical sorrow when Charlie inevitably packed back up and headed off again. The dog had died when Charlie was in the army, and he felt himself getting teary-eyed at the thought of the old dog dying without him. He realized he didn't even know where his parents had buried Duke. Now that he thought about it, his great-grandfather had also died while he was in Germany, and he wasn't sure where he was buried, either.

He wondered if great-grandfather Arlen's story about the tenant farmer had been true, or if he'd just made it up to scare Charlie and his brothers and sisters. Most of his anecdotes about his frontier youth were similarly sensational, filled with gory, petty violence, drunken cowboys, ubiquitous, terrible sickness, vengeful Indians and wandering ghosts. The old man would have been tickled at the idea of the three cadavers spending the winter together under the ice in Lake Bascomb, a murderer and his two victims waiting for the spring thaw.

At bottom Charlie was as disappointed to find out that Desiray had been sleeping with Vic regularly as he was to learn that he'd killed her. More than once she'd expressed a strong dislike for Vic, and he didn't see anything Vic could have done for her professionally that he couldn't or wouldn't have himself. She did have a pretty voracious appetite for coke. He remembered going home with her one summer night and watching her do line after line, becoming more and more manic as the night went on, punctuating her intake with glasses of jug wine and finishing off the evening with an enthusiastic blow job for Charlie. Now that he thought about it, if Vic was trading her coke for sex, his seemingly limitless supply of the former might have caused her to make the lethal mistake of speculating out loud to Vic about its source. Charlie had liked Desiray, liked her a lot, in fact, and for months he'd tried hard to pretend that her disappearance hadn't been what it had seemed. He was sorry that she was dead after all, sorry to know that Vic had done it, and now that he thought about it, he wasn't at all sorry he'd killed Vic.

*

He returned to the Cavanaugh residence without much hope of finding the money there. If Roy hadn't found it, it was most likely somewhere else. According to Dennis, Vic had stopped in at the Tease-O-Rama that afternoon, but there'd been too much chance of Charlie going back there for Vic to have risked using it to hide the money. After a cursory and unsuccessful search for any liquor he and Vic might have missed earlier he sat down at the kitchen table to think. On the counter next to it was an answering machine, its red light blinking on and off.

'Hello?' It was a woman's voice, husky and wary, and she said nothing else before she hung up, two or three seconds later. It sounded a lot like Renata, but after five playbacks Charlie still couldn't say for sure one way or the other. He picked up an address book from the scattered contents of an overturned kitchen drawer and looked up Renata's name. Her home number was there in Vic's childish hand, and Charlie started to dial it. He stopped and looked down again. Her home address was there, too. It was five-thirty. Whether he found the money or not, he was going to have to get out of town very soon.

*

Renata's house was a plain-looking white A-frame on a side street a mile west of the Sweet Cage. A light was on in the living room as he drove by. He parked the Mercedes down the street and walked up the sidewalk to her porch. The snow had stopped, and the neighborhood was perfectly still except for the crunch of his feet on the snowy sidewalk. He stepped onto the porch and rapped on the glass. A moment later a hand pulled the front window curtain back and Renata peered out at him, looking not the least surprised. She opened the door.

'Hello, Charlie.' She opened the door wide and he shouldered past her into the house. 'What brings you here? Hoping I might still reward you for your act of kindness toward me?' She shut the door behind her.

Her living room was warm and dim, her furniture old and worn. A fire burned in the fireplace. She had on tight pants, a clinging black turtleneck sweater and no shoes. Her bright red toenails showed through a filmy layer of nylon to match her long fingernails, and the detail aroused him slightly. Her hair was still pulled in a tight knot behind her head.

'Where were you? I went by the Sweet Cage after we talked and there was nobody there.'

'I couldn't sit there and wait for you any more, Charlie. You said you'd be by in twenty minutes.'

'A cop stopped me.' He was sure it hadn't been much

more than twenty, but there were other matters to attend to now. 'I heard your message.'

'What message?' She moved toward the kitchen and turned back to him, standing in the open doorway.

'You left a message on Vic's answering machine.'

'Why would I call Vic? I don't even have his phone number. Anyway, whenever I get one of those things I just hang up. I won't talk to a machine.'

'It was someone who sounded a lot like you, then.'

'Sounded like me? What did she say?'

'Just "hello", then she hung up.'

'It wasn't me. Did you ever find Vic?'

'Yeah, I found him. He's dead.'

She raised an eyebrow. 'Did Roy Gelles do it?'

'Roy's dead, too.'

'So you're free to go. Why stop over here?' She leaned back onto the frame of the kitchen door with her arms folded over her chest, an amused, slightly disdainful smile beginning to play at the corners of her mouth. It seemed to him she was consciously arching her back in order to accentuate her breasts.

'I can't find the money. I can't leave without it.'

'You think it's here?'

'I don't know. All I know is the voice on Vic's machine sounded like you.'

She shrugged. 'Look around if you like.'

He sat down at her dining-room table. 'I guess not. You have anything to drink?'

'Just coffee and tea.'

'No liquor?'

'Not even wine. You want some coffee? Yes or no.'

'I guess not.' His head throbbed, and the dull pain in his hip was constant now.

'Maybe the woman on the answering machine was Bonnie. She has a husky voice. You know, one of those booze and cigarette voices.'

'Vic and Bonnie haven't spoken in three years, as far as I know, except maybe to exchange insults.'

'As far as you know. Maybe she's got the money.' She sat down at the table next to him and leaned forward. 'She still lives in their old house, right?'

Charlie nodded. It seemed unlikely. Charlie had never seen a marriage break up with such animal viciousness as Vic and Bonnie's, not even his own.

'You don't suppose he was planning to take her and the kids with him all along, and cut you out of it, do you?'

'You got the last part right. He was planning to put me in Lake Bascomb.'

'Or if he wasn't taking her with him he might have just thought her house would be a safe place to stash the money until the morning.'

'It's possible.'

'Even if she's not in on it, isn't it possible he went over to see the kids? He might have some kind of hiding place there, maybe a floor safe or something.'

It began to make sense to him. Vic was no more attentive a father than he was, but Christmas would have presented him with the perfect excuse to go over there and hide something. 'He could have wrapped it up and put it under the tree.'

Renata nodded. 'How much money are we really

talking about, Charlie? If you were both planning to skip town on it, it's got to be a lot more than what you managed to skim off the top for a couple of years.'

'Yesterday at noon I cleaned out the operating accounts for the whole operation.'

'So that's, what, five or six businesses total? Let's say twelve grand, maybe fifteen. Still not nearly enough for you and Vic both to be planning to cash out on.'

Charlie sighed and stood. It was five-forty-five. 'We were running some coke on the side. A pretty fair amount of it, actually. Behind Bill's back.'

'Jesus Christ, Charlie. Bill Gerard would have cut off your skin in little pieces if he ever found out.'

'The idea was to get out of town after we'd made a lot of money but before he found out about it.'

'It's a lot of money, then.'

'It's a great big fucking pile of money. I'd better get over to Bonnie's before they come downstairs to open presents.'

She rose and moved toward him. 'If you want to come back here before you go, Charlie . . .' She put a hand on his shoulder and the other on his hip. They leaned together and kissed for a moment. Her mouth tasted like Doublemint gum masking tobacco, one of Charlie's favorite combinations. Then she pulled back, her palms flat on his chest, their fingers arched and their long red nails pressing through his overcoat and his shirt. 'You should get going now.' Her accent seemed slightly thicker than usual.

*

Ten minutes later he was sitting in the Mercedes across the street and three houses down from Bonnie's house in a newish subdivision of almost identical two-storey houses in an area that had been farmland when Charlie was growing up. He got out of the car and crossed the street, the edgy anticipation of the break-in diminished somewhat by the notion that hardly anyone would suspect a middle-aged, well-dressed white man driving a late model Mercedes of anything sinister in a neighborhood like this, even before six in the morning. That this was a man who had that very Christmas morning committed his first murder and was about to commit his first burglary would not have occurred to the casual observer.

He moved to the side of the house, where he brushed the snow from around a basement window. He sat down in the hollow he'd made and braced himself, knowing he could only afford the noise of a single kick. His right foot shot straight through the window, knocking his shoe loose at the heel and making what seemed to him to be an excessive amount of noise, but he sat motionless for thirty seconds with no indication he'd been heard. Carefully he extracted his foot from the cracked window, his shoe dangling from his toes, and as he pulled it out the shoe caught on an outcropping of broken glass and dropped into the basement. Cursing quietly he got onto his knees, stuck his hand in and managed to unlatch the window without gashing his wrist open.

He lowered himself quietly into the basement, his right sock soaked.

*

The almost perfect blackness was broken only by the pale grey rectangles of the windows where the walls met the ceiling. He felt his way to the wall and moved lopsidedly inch by inch around the room by touch, careful to avoid upsetting the storage boxes lining the walls, until he reached the stairs just opposite the windows. Moving his palm up and down the rough wall he located a lightswitch and flipped it on. The basement was unfinished, with mottled grey concrete walls and a smooth cement floor, stacked high with unused junk. A pair of bare bulbs glowed yellow in the ceiling fixture, one considerably dimmer than the other. He spent a minute looking around under the broken window for his shoe without success, bewildered, quietly moving aside boxes of old clothes and toys. He searched the rest of the room for two or three minutes before giving up on it. He turned out the light and moved slowly up the stairs.

The kitchen was only marginally brighter than the basement. He pulled open the refrigerator door, holding onto the body of it with his right hand to steady himself and minimize the dull pop of the separating rubber doorseal. He leaned down and found no beer or wine inside, just a large assortment of soft drinks, fruit juice and milk, and he moved on.

The tree was a big one, standing in the far corner of the living room, with a good thirty brightly wrapped packages scattered beneath it. He knelt to examine them and found that he was unable to make out the writing on the tags in the dark. He crawled around to the back of the tree, found the end of the light cord and plugged it into the wall. The multicolored lights cast a surprisingly bright, soft light on the room, and on the coffee table he saw a plate of partially eaten cookies and a half-empty glass of milk; at least he wouldn't have to worry about Bonnie coming down to play Santa. On the mantle above the fireplace hung three filled Christmas stockings beneath a multitude of framed family photos, including one, surprisingly enough, of Vic. Charlie doubted very much that his own photo was to be found anywhere in Sarabeth's house, unless Melissa had one hidden away somewhere. The names on the packages were clearly legible now, and he began sorting through them. The first package he found with Vic's handwriting on the tag was a big box addressed 'To: Nina. From: Daddy.' He dug at the ends of the scotch tape with the ends of his fingernails, trying and failing not to tear the paper beneath in the process. When he peeled the wrapping paper from the top he saw the words 'LITTLE BABY CHEWYFACE' and under those the recommendation that the toy was for children from four to eight. He pulled the top of the box open and inside it found Little Baby ChewyFace, some instructions and nothing else. He remembered the doll well, having given one to Melissa two or three years earlier when it had been the hot item of the moment. When the child put baby food in its mouth the doll seemed to chew, particles of food actually dribbled out the sides of its mouth, and at some point the child's mother had to clean the doll. It performed several other more or less disgusting and high-mainten-ance functions as well, and Melissa had seemed pleased enough with hers at the time. He replaced the doll in the box and repaired the wrapping as best he could, then set about looking for more of Vic's packages. He'd found one marked 'To: Danny. From: Dad' and was about to open it when it occurred to him that even Vic wouldn't have left a present for one of his children that he'd have to take away before Christmas morning rolled around. The money would have to be in a box addressed to Bonnie.

But where was it? Jesus, these people gave each other lots of presents. To Mommy from Susy. To Danny from Nina. To Susy from Santa. Every possible combination except to Bonnie from Vic. He pressed on. Grandma and Grandpa, uncles, aunts and cousins, all of them presumably Bonnie's side of the family. And there in the corner, right next to where he'd grabbed the light cord from the carpet, sat a large package wrapped in the same green paper as Little Baby ChewyFace. He picked it up and hoisted it over the other packages. Its considerable weight was unevenly distributed within, and he set it down in front of him and flipped open the tag. 'To: my one and only BONNIE, With hope for the Future. From: Vic.'

He drew a sharp breath and was ready to take the package out the door when a tiny voice stopped him.

'You're not Santa.'

He looked over his shoulder and saw a dark-haired little girl of five or six, dressed in Smurf pajamas and staring at him with fierce loathing.

He rose to his feet and bent over at the waist, fingers arched on his knees. He whispered his reply, shushing as he raised his right hand and placed its index finger to his lips. 'I'm one of his helpers. And you must be Nina.'

'I'm Susy,' she said out loud, condescending. 'Nina's almost twelve.'

'Oh, that's right.' Presumably Nina was going to be disappointed with Baby ChewyFace, then. 'You're such a big girl, I mistook you for your big sister. Ho, ho, ho.'

'What's your name?' Her expression didn't soften.

'Charlie.'

'What are you doing here?'

'Just making sure all the packages are addressed to the right people.'

'You're stealing our presents.'

'You're going to wake everyone up. You don't want to do that, do you?'

'I don't care. It's almost morning anyway.'

'How old are you, Susy?'

'I'm five.' She pointed to the package. 'That's from my dad to my mom. Put it back.'

Charlie looked down at the tag and affected surprise. 'So it is, so it is.' He put it next to the tree, outside the circle of presents.

'Not there. Where it was. In the back.'

He picked it up again and placed it carefully back in its original spot. 'There we go. Well, I guess I'm about ready to head back to the North Pole. Maybe you ought to go back to bed until it's really morning.'

She stared at him, unconvinced. 'I'm too excited to sleep.'

'If you don't give it a try I'll have to tell Santa. He wouldn't like that.'

'You don't know Santa.'

'That's what you think.'

'How come you only have one shoe?'

'The other one fell out of the sleigh.'

'Okay,' the little girl sighed, looking resigned, and she turned away from him. For a moment he thought he'd pulled it off, and then she called out over her shoulder. 'I'm going to go tell my mom.'

Charlie knelt, picked up the package and ran into the darkness of the kitchen to the accompaniment of an earsplitting shriek from little Susy, knocking against the sharp corner of a low counter with his sore hip. He wrestled with the back-door deadbolt.

'Mommy! A guy's stealing our presents! Mommy!' Her voice had the tone of a rocksaw cutting marble. He threw the door open and sprinted as well as he could manage one-shoed through the snow back to the Mercedes. He threw the package onto the passenger seat and turned the engine over, and as he pulled out and away he saw a light come on upstairs.

*

A mile away he thought he heard a siren in the distance. He pulled into a supermarket parking lot, turned the headlights off and sat under a lamppost with the engine running. The siren was getting close, howling louder and louder until a police cruiser materialized and blew a red light through the intersection in the general direction of Bonnie's house. Charlie was relieved that there were a few early morning churchgoers on the streets. He didn't know if Bonnie had seen the Mercedes out her window or not, but in any case it seemed best from now on not to be pretty much the only car on the road.

It was time he got back to Renata's, but first he wanted to take a look at the money. He tore eagerly at the green paper and found a cardboard box ducttaped firmly shut and marked on two sides with a Miller High Life logo. After a failed attempt to loosen the tape with his thumbnail he shut the engine off and tore at the tape lengthwise with the car key. The tape split wide open down the center and he pulled up on the sideflaps with a loud ripping sound as the tape on the sides separated from the box. Inside, orange from the light spilling in from the lamppost, were balls of wadded newspaper, and he fished through them until his hand touched something solid. He pulled out a wooden block the size and shape of a blackboard eraser. He began tossing the crumpled newspaper pages onto the floor of the passenger side, followed by another dozen or so of the wooden blocks, until he came to a hand-printed note on a piece of yellow legal paper at the bottom:

> Merry Christmas BITCH!
> Good BYE. VIC.

Stunned, he leaned forward and took several deep breaths to avert panic, gripping the wheel so hard his fingers started to hurt. He had almost no money. Maybe Renata would be willing to front him enough to get out of town. With great deliberation he managed to place the blocks and newspaper back in the box and set it down on the parking lot next to the car, and then he drove away, the pedals hard-edged and hard to hold down under his wet, shoeless right sock.

*

Again he parked the Mercedes down the street from Renata's house and limped slowly toward it, his hip worse than ever, the pain in his skull throbbing to the time of his heartbeat. When he got inside he'd take her up on her earlier offer of coffee, maybe ask if she had an aspirin.

He rang the bell and waited. No one came. The screen door was slightly ajar, and he opened it and tried the doorknob. It gave and he pushed his way inside. The lights were still on in the living room and the kitchen, and the house was quiet.

'Renata?' There was no response Next to a chair by the fireplace an oddly colored paperback lay split open, pages facing down, a title in a language Charlie didn't recognize running along its cracked spine. In the fireplace the fire still burned, and the newest of the logs hadn't been going long. He moved down the back hallway, calling her name.

To his left was a half-open door. Inside the room was dark, and he moved uncertainly by the faraway light from the living room to a frilly table lamp on a nightstand. Turning it on he saw that under it was a lace doily. Renata's bed was an antique four-poster, covered with a quilt that might have been a hundred years old. The walls were covered with family photos, many of them in recognizably local settings – one was a group photo taken sometime in the 1930s at some company's Fourth of July picnic at Lake Bascomb, the dock clearly visible in the background. Not one of the photos included Renata, and in fact nothing here seemed to Charlie as though it really belonged to her. It was as though she had rented the house fully furnished with the sentimental relics of someone else's life and brought nothing with her that might betray the tenant's actual identity but her clothes and a few indecipherable foreign paperbacks.

The back of the house was locked tight. Down a rickety flight of wooden stairs he found the basement completely empty except for a sump pump and a hot water heater. Slowly he made his way back up the stairs. Renata was gone, almost certainly with his money, and his range of options was narrowing further with every passing second.

CHAPTER FIFTEEN

Again he parked around the corner and approached the Sweet Cage on foot, putting as little weight as possible on the shoeless right one with each step in case of broken glass hidden by the snow. The only car in the parking lot was a black 1980 Lincoln Continental, and for a brief, disoriented moment he thought it was his own company car. On closer examination he realized his mistake; this Lincoln had out of state plates. It was Bill Gerard's own car. There was no one inside.

Two sets of fresh footprints, one male from the driver's side and one female from the other, led from the Lincoln to the side door. They looked to him to be the only prints made since the snow had stopped. Charlie went first to the side door and tried it very gently. It was locked, and so was the front door. He looked at the pay phone on the corner and tried to come up with a legitimate excuse he could use for needing to get into the Sweet Cage outside business hours. Nothing remotely convincing suggested itself, but he moved over to the phone anyway and dialed information.

'Have you got a listing for a Sidney McCallum?'

'I have an S.J. McCallum on Tennessee and a D.S. on Twenty-third.'

'Give me both of them.'

He tried S.J. McCallum on Tennessee first. S.J. turned out to be a young woman who objected violently to being awakened before dawn on Christmas morning, and though she wasn't Sidney, the torrent of abuse that came flowing over the line at Charlie was vivid and raunchy enough to suggest some sort of kinship with him. D.S. on Twenty-third stood for D. Sidney McCallum, and when he picked up he hadn't been to bed yet.

'I can't help it, I'm still pissed off about my mom and her husband just up and taking off for the Garden of the goddamn Gods with no warning and leaving me with my kids. Plus which that asshole boyfriend of Rusti's tonight really got my adrenalin going.'

'I thought you were supposed to get tired after a big adrenalin rush like that.'

'Well, I'm not. So what's up?'

'I got no place to go. Can I come over?'

This caught Sidney off guard. 'Yeah. That'd be good, I got something to talk to you about anyway. I could make you some eggs and coffee if you want. Kids won't be up for a couple hours, hopefully.' Charlie wrote down the address and limped back to the Mercedes as fast as he could.

*

Five minutes later Sidney let him into his house. 'Sorry it's such a mess. We don't have anybody over, usually.' It was disorderly but clean, with toys as the predominant factor in the disorder. Charlie looked around the room for a key rack as Sidney led him back to the kitchen. 'So, you just been out wandering around?'

'Yeah, more or less.'

'I do that sometimes, after I get off. Nights when I don't have the kids, anyway. Just get out there and drive around with no particular destination.' He looked down at Charlie's sock. 'Looks like you lost a shoe, there.'

'Yeah.' He didn't offer an explanation and hoped Sidney wouldn't press it.

'You want to borrow some boots or something? What size are you?'

'Nine.'

'I'm a thirteen wide. Sorry.' He opened a cabinet. 'I can make some coffee, if you want some.'

'I'd rather have a drink, if that's okay.' There was no key rack in the kitchen, either.

'I don't think I've got anything. I don't drink at home much, because of the kids . . .' As Sidney opened the refrigerator Charlie was vastly relieved to see two bottles of Schlitz inside the door. 'Hey, what do you know, you're in luck.' Sidney pulled out one of the bottles and cracked the cap off on the edge of the counter.

Charlie took it from him gratefully and held it before his eyes. Two 3.2 beers wouldn't stop the pain in his head, but it would do something towards taking the edge off.

'I think I'll join you, come to think of it,' Sidney said, reaching for the other one, and Charlie's heart broke a little as the big man cracked the second bottle open for himself. He took a first expectant sip of his own and his heart broke a little more as he realized that the bottle must have been in the refrigerator for a year or more. The beer was sour and lifeless, bitter as fermented aspirin, but he tried to convince himself that he could get it down. He swallowed the tiny sip with some difficulty.

'Here's to next year, Charlie,' Sidney said, and took a giant swig that reversed course before it got to his throat, spraying the door of the refrigerator and Charlie's overcoat with spoiled beer. 'Shit! Gone skunky on me. Told you I don't drink much at home. Yours okay?'

'Yeah, it's a little flat, but it's okay,' he said as he took a running shot at another sip. This one tasted worse than the first, and he set the bottle down next to the sink, admitting defeat. 'On second thought, it is kind of skunky.'

Sidney shook his massive head sadly and poured both bottles foamlessly into the sink. 'I'll make some coffee anyway. You go on into the living room and sit down.'

*

Charlie sat down on the living room couch and looked around, trying to picture where the keys might be if they weren't in Sidney's pants pocket. If they were, Charlie had no idea what he'd do. The options seemed limited to knocking Sidney cold when he wasn't expecting it, or asking him nicely if he could please borrow the keys for a couple of hours. Neither possibility held much promise. After a couple of minutes Sidney came out of the kitchen, set a cup of coffee in front of Charlie and sat down in a recliner opposite.

'So you're probably wondering what I wanted to talk

to you about.' Until that moment Charlie had forgotten that Sidney had mentioned something he wanted to discuss.

'Yeah. So, what's on your mind?'

'You think that kid's gonna press charges?'

'I don't know. I doubt it.' He hadn't thought about it.

'I can't believe I did it. Makes me sick to my stomach. Feels like a fucking hangover. But he was going after her with a tire iron, Charlie. A fucking tire iron. And that new boyfriend of hers was no fucking help at all. He was curled up there in a fetal position *whimpering* while this guy smashed his driver's side window and came after him and Rusti.' He shook his head. 'But still. I don't know why I couldn't have just fucked him up a little and sent him on his way. Those hands of his are crippled for life, probably.'

'I thought that was the idea. Him being a guitar player.'

Sidney smiled a little at the thought. 'Yeah.'

'Look at it this way. It'll make it harder for him to beat anybody up.'

'Yeah. When I think about Rusti's black eye I don't feel so bad. But that's not really what gets me, Charlie. It's the principle. I just don't believe in solving problems with force all the time any more. Karma and all that shit.'

'But you're a bouncer.'

'You'd be surprised how many troublemakers'll walk away quietly with a warning. It's all in the voice. And the intensity of the stare.'

'Sure, I've seen you do it. But sometimes the stare doesn't cut it.'

'I know, I know. So what do you think the odds are there'll be charges filed?'

'Who knows. I know the cops pretty well who took him to the emergency room, and they weren't any more impressed with him than you were, so I doubt they'll cause you any trouble. He was delirious when they took him away.'

'You ever handled an assault case, Charlie?'

'No. You'll have to get yourself a criminal lawyer if he files charges himself, but I'd be real surprised if he did. Does he know you?'

'Kind of. He knows I'm the bartender at the Sweet Cage.'

Charlie wrote a name and number down on a Marlboro ad on the back of a *TV Guide* on the coffee table in front of him. 'Call this guy if it comes up. Tell him the whole story, don't leave anything out, and he'll have the kid's ass in a legal sling. Nothing to worry about.'

He tested the temperature of the coffee with a measured sip, then took a long drink. It was hard for Charlie to concentrate on anything but what was happening back at the Sweet Cage. The way he figured it, Bill Gerard and Renata were at that very moment going through his money. His money. Some of it was stolen from Bill, true, but most of it he and Vic had earned fair and square.

The big man sighed and stood up. 'You want some scrambled eggs? I'm gonna have some.'

'Sure,' Charlie said, and Sidney went back into the kitchen. Charlie stuck his hands into his overcoat pocket and fingered his own keys, and as he sat jingling them it came to him. He had a distinct mental image of Sidney at the Sweet Cage going to his coat hanging behind the bar to get his keys; he kept them in his overcoat pocket so he'd always know where to find them. He went to the closet by the front door and opened it. He looked through it, trying to figure out which of the coats was the right one.

'Oh, sorry,' Sidney said from the kitchen doorway. 'I should've taken it when you first walked in the door. Like I said, we don't have people over very often.' Charlie smiled stiffly and took his own overcoat off to hang it up, as though that had been his intention all along. 'I was just going to ask if you wanted three eggs or four.'

'Three, I guess.'

Sidney returned to the kitchen and Charlie saw the coat hanging at the far end of the rack. He stuck his hand into one pocket, then the other. In the second pocket was a large key ring. Quietly he slipped the keys into his own coat pocket and turned toward the front door.

Again Sidney appeared in the kitchen door. 'Can't find a hanger?'

'No, I found one.' He took the coat off and hung it in the closet as Sidney returned to the kitchen.

'Another minute and they're done.'

If he bolted there was always a chance Sidney would follow and get the keys back, and he'd never get into the Sweet Cage without them. He sat back down on the couch and flipped through the TV Guide, telling himself that Bill and Renata had a lot to hash out and would thus still be at the Sweet Cage on his return. The TV Guide was full of ads for the same cartoon Christmas specials he'd had to watch over and over, year after year when he lived with Sarabeth and the kids. He could still practically recite dialogue from some of them.

Sidney stepped out of the kitchen with two plates of greyish scrambled eggs and set them down on the coffee table with a bottle of Tabasco sauce.

Charlie took a bite of the ashen scrambled eggs, noting something crusty and old sticking to a tine of the fork. The eggs were bland, and he shook a considerable portion of the Tabasco on them.

'How are the eggs?'

'Good, thanks,' he said, and with the addition of the Tabasco it was almost the truth.

'I feel a lot better about all this, Charlie. I owe you one.'

'No you don't. The eggs are enough.' Charlie hadn't realized it, but he really had been hungry. If he had any more time to spare he would have asked Sidney for more, but as soon as the plate was empty he stood up, leaving the plate on the table.

'I guess I'd better get going, then,' he said.

'Yeah, I should get a couple hours' sleep before the kids wake up.'

It occurred to Charlie that he had no idea how many kids Sidney had, nor anything else about them. 'Wish them a merry Christmas from me.'

'I will, buddy. Merry Christmas to you, too. You're a real friend, you know that?' Sidney got him in a tight bear hug that actually hurt his sides. 'Be seeing you soon.'

He opened the door and Charlie headed back to the Mercedes.

'Hey, got rid of the Lincoln, huh?'

'Company car,' Charlie said as he got in.

*

He pulled into the Sweet Cage lot and parked perpendicular to Bill Gerard's Lincoln, almost touching it, so that Bill wouldn't be able to leave without moving the Mercedes or damaging both vehicles. Charlie didn't stop to ask himself exactly what he intended to accomplish with this maneuver, but he felt resourceful doing it. He stepped out and looked at the snow. There were the same two pairs of footprints leading into the building, along with his own from earlier, and no new ones beside his leading away from either door. At the front door he tried three of the keys on Sidney's ring before he found the one that slid into the lock and turned. He pushed the door open slowly, made relatively certain the dark front room was empty, slipped inside and pulled the door quietly shut behind him. The light behind the bar was on, and so was one in Renata's office to its side. He crept along the wall opposite, listening for voices. Hearing none, he approached Renata's office.

From inside he could make out the sound of Renata's breathing. She sounded as though she were laboring at something. He pulled Roy Gelles's little gun from the inside pocket of his overcoat and pushed the door open.

Renata looked up at him from behind her desk, her hands underneath it. 'You're just full of surprises tonight, Charlie,' she said, her voice low.

He gestured with the revolver. 'Let's get those hands where I can see 'em.'

'Don't be a fucking idiot. Keep your voice down. You watch too many stupid old movies.'

He aimed the empty gun at her face. 'I want to see your hands on the desk.'

'I can't. Look.' With her head she gestured for him to move around the desk, and with some misgivings he did. Her hands were cuffed to its leg, forcing her to sit leaning forward.

'Bill did this?'

'You're a genius, Charlie.'

'Shit. Where is he? What if he comes back? This thing's not loaded.' The gangster movie aspect of the situation that had thrilled him moments ago had lost its appeal.

'He's taking a dump.'

'Where are the keys?'

'I don't know. His pocket, probably.'

'It doesn't matter. I'll lift the desk and you can slip the handcuffs out from around the leg. We can get out before he gets done in there.'

'Not yet. He's got your money.'

'How'd he get that?'

'I don't know.'

'Well, it sure wasn't under Bonnie's tree.'

'He came by the house with it a few minutes after you left. He accused me of being in on it with Vic.'

'Just Vic? Not me?'

'He wasn't very clear on anybody else but Vic. He's been trying to get me to talk.'

'How?'

'Pull back the collar of my sweater.' He reached down

and pulled at it, and she winced. Three circular red welts marked the right side of her neck.

'Jesus, are those cigarette burns?' He noted an odor of freshly smoked tobacco in the room.

She nodded, without a discernible trace of self-pity. 'There's a shotgun under the bar. You know how to use one?'

'Lot better than I do one of these things.' He put Roy's gun back in his overcoat pocket.

'Go get it and wait. When he comes back in here, wait until I say "All right, I'll tell you what I know." That's your signal you've got a clear shot.'

'I'll be outside, behind the stage,' he said. She nodded.

*

The shotgun lay easily handy on a shelf below the front bar. Charlie pulled it out and took a good long time opening the breech to avoid any audible clicks that might carry to Gerard's stall. It was loaded and ready. He took an extra handful of shells from a small box next to where the shotgun had been and dropped them into his coat pocket. He hadn't fired a gun of any kind since the army, and didn't think he'd fired a shotgun since he was a teenager. He tried to think of the last thing he'd shot, but couldn't put his finger on it. Maybe a duck, or more likely quail. He'd never been too keen on getting up before dawn to go sit in a fetid duck blind and wait for the ducks to come. He closed the breech and carried the gun, barrel up, to the small circular stage. A first attempt to kneel behind the stage brought on another terrible burst of pain in his hip, and he ended up lying on his side, ready to rise when Gerard crossed from the men's room to Renata's office.

His free hand brushed against something soft on the floor, and he picked up what he recognized as Amy Sue's blue panties. He wondered why she hadn't put them back on after her last dance, then decided he didn't want or need to know. He rubbed the silky material between his fingers for a second, then hooked one of its legs over the barrel of the gun and began twirling it in a circular motion, watching the shiny blue panties gyrate in the cold, stale air of the club.

He stopped when he heard a toilet flushing, barely noticing as the panties slid midway down the barrel. He clicked the safety off and peered around the corner of the stage. The men's room door opened and Bill Gerard strutted tall and potbellied out of it, buckling his belt, his normally immaculate silver hair a disheveled mess. Over his arm was draped the jacket of a brown three-piece suit, its vest hanging unbuttoned from his narrow shoulders. Even thirty feet away Charlie could see he had an erection and needed a shave. He followed Bill's head with the end of the barrel, leading it just slightly. When the moment came to pull the trigger, Bill surprised him by yelling, and the moment was lost.

'You know what really pisses me off,' he bellowed into the office. 'I'm going to miss my grandkids opening their presents this morning if I don't get on the road soon. And by the time I get back I'll be exhausted.'

He disappeared into the office and Charlie rose awkwardly and painfully to his feet. He heard Renata's voice, but he couldn't make out what she was saying.

Bill Gerard had stopped yelling, but even at a normal conversational tone his nasal, braying voice was loud enough to hear from Charlie's position.

'So how much longer are you going to keep me here on Christmas?' Charlie was twenty feet from the door. 'Seems to me we could clear this up pretty easy if you decide to talk to me.'

Renata said something, but Charlie couldn't hear what it was.

'Fair enough. Now you know what I want you to do for me? I want you to open that pretty little red mouth of yours, and when you've learnt who's in charge here maybe you'll be a little more forthcoming with the information I require.'

Charlie couldn't make out Renata's reply, but he was close enough now to see through the doorway. Gerard had pulled his cock out of his fly and was holding it, erect, inches from Renata's expressionless face. She showed no sign that she saw Charlie standing outside the door behind Gerard.

'Now open up for Bill,' Gerard said, and he moved a little closer to Renata as Charlie drew a bead on his head. 'Come on, goddamnit, I'm not funning here.'

Gerard's head was fifteen feet from the end of the barrel. Charlie hesitated. Pretend it's a duck. A motionless, curly-haired duck with a hard-on. He squeezed the trigger and the gun went off, prompting a startled yelp of pain from Gerard and a speckling of red spots against the white of his hair instead of the explosion of skull and brains Charlie had anticipated.

'What the fuck...' Gerard's voice was up an octave as

he turned around, his cock still in his hand. 'Charlie? Jesus, the one guy down here I thought I could trust.' He took a look at the shotgun. 'A four ten? You tried to kill me with a fucking four ten loaded for *snake?* I don't know whether to laugh or be insulted.'

'Don't move, Bill.' Charlie advanced on Gerard. 'That was just to get your attention. At this range I'll kill you dead.'

Gerard smirked, let go of his dick and reached into his vest. He came out with a .22 caliber pistol and waved it at Charlie. 'You really shit in your nest now, Charlie. Now set that fucking thing down.'

Charlie still had a bead on Bill Gerard's head, and he tried hard not to glance down at Renata, who had discreetly moved off the chair and onto her knees, her head within striking distance of Gerard's cock, still semi-erect and swinging.

'You half-assed farthammer, you haven't even got both your shoes on. Come on, Charlie. I want to hear what all you've done to betray my trust before I shoot you. I want the details. I want . . .' Gerard's voice cracked, his eyes went wide and he dropped the pistol. 'Oh, sweet Jesus . . .' Charlie finally allowed himself to glance down at Renata and found her with her mouth around Gerard's joint, though not the way he'd intended. She had a good sideways grip on his shaft, her teeth bared and poised to bite it right into three separate pieces. Bill's momentary panic returned quickly enough to rage, and he placed the barrel of the .22 against Renata's right orbital bone. 'If I even get the idea you're thinking about biting down, you're gonna be minus an eye.'

Charlie took three quick steps forward and fired, the end of the barrel less than a foot and a half from Gerard's face. Snakeshot from the four ten tore into it and Gerard fell backward. Renata released her grip, pulled away and watched as he hit the ground, his face dotted with tiny, oddly clean holes that pooled quickly with blood and began overflowing as he lay there, raggedly sucking in air.

'I helped you a lot, Charlie. Goddamn.' His voice was sticky, his throat filling with liquid.

'Charlie!' She barked it, and there was no question of who was in charge. 'Pick up the fucking pistol and finish him.'

He picked the pistol up off the floor and aimed it at Bill Gerard's pocked, oozing face. Bill didn't look like he much cared what Charlie did next. 'He's dying anyway.'

'Take that pillow and put it over his face.'

He picked up a green velvet throw pillow from a chair in the corner of the office and placed it over Gerard's face as ordered. He didn't resist; in fact he seemed only vaguely aware of Charlie's presence. Charlie pressed the muzzle into the pillow and fired. The sound wasn't too bad, he thought, but he started to worry about the noise the shotgun blasts had made. He almost lifted the pillow, then changed his mind. Renata looked coolly down at him.

'Why didn't you tell me it was a four ten? I almost got us both killed, firing at him from that distance.'

'That's why I told you to wait until I said "I'll tell you what I know."'

'I couldn't hear what you were saying from out there.

Anyway if I'd waited any longer he'd have had his dick in your mouth.'

'So fucking what? It ended up there anyway, didn't it? The idea was for me to blow him until his guard was down, then I'd give the signal and you could get close enough to kill him.' She shook her head in wonderment at his inability to follow the simplest of instructions.

Charlie sighed. 'In order to give me the signal, you'd have had to interrupt the blow job and he would've heard me.'

'I wouldn't have said it until after he came.'

'What the hell are you doing with a pop gun like that behind the bar anyway? Loaded with *snake*shot, for Christ's sake?'

'Sidney's in charge of all that. He doesn't want to kill anybody.'

'From a liability point of view, that's pretty stupid, Renata. You'd both be in a lot more legal hot water for Sidney maiming somebody than for killing him.'

'Well, now I know.'

'So where's the money?'

She nodded at a satchel like an old-fashioned doctor's bag sitting on the floor of the office. Charlie picked it up and set it on the desk. 'Go ahead and open it. Bill already showed me.'

Charlie took a deep breath. He undid the latches and opened the bag.

'How much money is it, Charlie?'

He almost wept at the sight of all the stacks of Franklins jumbled together in the satchel, held together with rubber bands. 'It's a whole lot of money.' On top of the pile was an envelope containing two plane tickets, in the names of G. and B. Newman. He tossed the .22 onto the pile with a little prayer of thanks. Bill Gerard had saved his plan.

'Is it enough to take me with you, or are you going to kill me, too?'

He looked up at her, stunned. 'I'm not going to kill you.'

'A man's just had his brains scrambled by a .22 caliber slug on my office floor, Charlie. It's going to make it difficult for me to stay in business. It's going to be a neat trick just staying out of jail. Looks like you've got a lot more than this club is worth in that bag of yours. If you're not going to take me along, I'd just as soon you killed me.'

'I'm not going to kill you.'

'Take me with you, then. I'd make it worth your while. I can be a *lot* of fun, Charlie.'

He looked at the tickets. Next to them in the envelope was an itinerary and invoice indicating that they had been paid for in cash. Neither G. nor B. Newman had been assigned a full name or gender. They could be Mr. and Mrs. Gregory Newman. He had the name and address of a document artisan in New York who would supply him in two days' time with a fake passport, and paying for another for Renata was easy enough. The very fact that there were two tickets in the bag was proof that Vic had planned to bring a woman along with him, anyway, wasn't it? The possibility lurked in the back of his mind that he'd been wrong about Vic's plans, but he didn't entertain it long.

'All right. You can come with me.'

Bill Gerard had more than saved his plan. He had made Charlie's fondest fantasy come true, a fantasy he'd never even articulated to himself, but there it was, buried in the depths of his unconscious brain: him and Renata, in the tropics somewhere, screwing on top of his big pile of money with a fully stocked wet bar next to it.

'Pick up the desk, then.'

Charlie lifted the corner of the desk, the pain in his hip masked by euphoria. 'You think anyone heard the shots?'

'Probably not,' she said, pulling the chain of the cuffs clear of the leg. 'We're pretty well insulated for sound because of the music. The four ten's not that loud for a shotgun, and you got a pretty good muffle on the .22 with the pillow. It's probably best not to hang around any longer than we have to, though. Now why don't you dig in his pocket for the key to the handcuffs and we'll go to my house and I'll pack a bag.'

He knelt down and stuck his hand in Bill Gerard's pants pocket. The body twitched once, almost imperceptibly, when he touched it, and in a panic Charlie yanked the gory pillow away from its face. The wounds were no longer bleeding.

'Don't worry, he's dead. Just find the key.'

Again he slipped his hand into the pocket and pulled out Bill's wallet, then an overloaded key ring, which he tossed to Renata.

'He's not going to keep handcuff keys on the same ring as his house keys, now, is he? Check his shirt pocket.'

In the shirt pocket was a tiny pair of keys on a small wire ring. He opened the cuffs and she again pulled the collar of her sweater away from the burns. 'I'd better get some antibiotic on these. Come on, let's get going.'

'Could I get a beer before we go?'

She reached into her bottom drawer and handed him a bottle of Johnny Walker Black. 'Here. We'll take it back to my place.'

'Hold on a second.' Charlie knelt again by Gerard's feet and pulled off his shoes. Size eleven. He took off his one shoe and both socks and put on Bill's dry socks, then tried on the left shoe, a burgundy wingtip. It fit better than his own. He put the other one on and took a walk around the room. His remaining problems seemed small.

CHAPTER SIXTEEN

It would take at least two and a half hours driving south to get to the airport, depending on the condition of the roads, but the eleven AM to New York was still a reasonable possibility, and if they missed it there would be others. He toyed with the possibility of getting a couple of first-class upgrades.

This time he parked the car right in Renata's driveway. The sun wasn't up yet, but the sky was lightening to a chalky grey as they came in through her back door.

*

'You wait in the living room while I pack, Charlie.'

He went in and sat down by the fireplace, placing the satchel safely at his feet. Again he picked up Renata's paperback and tried to make out the language. The alphabet was roman but there were odd characters and accents scattered throughout the text, and he found no place-name on the copyright page that corresponded to any city he knew. The paper was cheap and brittle, and a number of the pages were coming loose from the glue where she'd cracked the spine. On the cover was an amateurish painting of a farmer and his wife looking bravely out into the hazy future, suggesting a Soviet bloc origin – Hungary? Poland? Lithuania?

'No time to screw, I don't think, but if you feel like it I'll blow you before we get going,' she yelled from the bedroom. Her accent was a shade more pronounced than usual, as though she sensed he was speculating on her origins. 'In the meantime, why don't you fix yourself a drink?'

He looked down at the satchel. Inside was the Johnny Walker Black. He decided to wait until after the blow job and stood up. She was standing over an open suitcase on the bed. 'Are you leaving the photos?'

She looked back at the framed photographs as though she'd forgotten they were there. 'They're not mine.'

'Whose are they?'

'How do I know? Why don't you wait in the living room.'

'Where are you from, Renata? Originally.'

'Why are you asking me questions, Charlie? What's it got to do with anything?'

'I was just curious. I always wondered where you came from.'

'It's a long story. We've got plenty of time to get better acquainted, don't you think?'

'Yeah.' He went back to the chair by the fire, opened the satchel and twisted the cap of the Johnny Walker Black, tearing the tax stamp. His eye was drawn to the .22. Was the safety on? Did a .22 pistol even have a safety? He set the bottle down and picked up the pistol. Before tonight he'd never killed anyone in his life, and now he'd killed two. Three, if you counted helping Vic kill Roy Gelles. Call it two and a half. He wondered between the three of them how many people Vic, Roy and Bill had killed over the years. There wasn't a single incident he could name with any certainty, except for Vic killing Desiray. Bill Gerard was supposed to have beaten one of his streetwalkers to death with his bare fists once for talking back, but Charlie had always suspected that the story had been exaggerated or even concocted wholesale to impress and frighten Bill's colleagues and competition alike. In the end, Bill had turned out to be pretty easy to kill, even for a beginner. He weighed the pistol in his palm, thinking how close it had come to ending his life. A simple nervous reflex stemming from the shock of Renata's teeth clamping down on the shaft of Bill's penis had saved Charlie and Renata both from a bullet.

He dropped the .22 back into the satchel and was starting to picture the blow job when Renata's plan came back to him with nauseating clarity: the idea had been for her to blow Bill and kill him while his guard was down. He looked around the corner past the fireplace, back toward the bedroom. Renata's going away with him made no sense for her. Depending on his or anyone's generosity for her survival wasn't in her nature.

Fucking idiot. He set the bottle down again and approached the bedroom door.

'I'm almost done, Charlie. Go back and sit down.'

'I just wanted to ask you something.'

She stopped and looked up at him. 'What?'

He didn't really have a specific question planned. 'Nothing. Sorry.'

'Go back and sit down. I'll be done in a second and then I'll come in and give you a blow job like you've never had in your life.'

He went back to the living room and sat down. He picked the .22 back up and waited. He'd almost allowed his giddy relief at getting the money back and the inconceivably beautiful prospect of a life with a spectacular, unattainable woman to cloud his good judgment. Renata had been in on it with Vic, and she'd most likely called the cops to report the burglary at Bonnie's house. He had more than a quarter of a million dollars in a satchel, and he'd nearly traded it for a blow job that he wouldn't have lived to see the end of.

He listened to her in the bedroom, singing a song he couldn't identify. She had to be armed in some way. His only tactical advantage was her continuing belief that he was under her power.

'Almost done, Charlie,' she called. 'You want me naked or in some kind of sexy underwear?'

Either way might have weakened his resolve. 'Fully clothed.'

'What, like the suit I had on yesterday?'

That would have been even worse. He closed his eyes. 'Whatever you've got on now. We're running low on time.'

'Whatever you want, Charlie.'

He got up and moved across the room. He stood in the shadows near the kitchen door with the pistol.

'How long do you think we'll be in New York? Two, three days? Then we're out of the country? Charlie?'

She stopped by the fireplace, looking back toward the

bathroom, and he raised the pistol. She was beautiful. Her face was softer than he'd ever seen it. It was almost sweet. 'Charlie?' She chuckled, as though his absence signaled a game. She turned toward the bedroom, brow furrowed in playful curiosity. 'Are you back there? Did you double back on me?' As she disappeared from sight he lowered the pistol. He followed her into the hallway.

'Charlie?' She had her head stuck into the bedroom, one leg outstretched into the hallway for balance. Now was the time, while he couldn't see her face. Pretend she's a duck. He fired, the sound cracking through the little house like a cherrybomb, and Renata fell into the doorframe, a small wet spot on the back of her black sweater. She let out a quiet gasp as she slid to the oak floor. She turned enough as she did so to face Charlie when she hit the ground.

'What the fuck did you do that for? I think you hit me in the lung. Jesus, Charlie, call a doctor. Jesus. Jesus.'

'I'm sorry,' Charlie said, taking aim again, and he was. The second shot seemed louder than the first, and he knew he'd have to get out in a hurry this time. It, too, hit her in the chest.

'Why, Charlie, why?' The uncomprehending sorrow in her face and voice made him momentarily sure he'd made the wrong decision, but there was no changing it now.

'I'm sorry,' he said again.

'Call an ambulance.'

'You know I can't do that.'

'Then sit here and hold me,' she whimpered.

He knelt down beside her, intending to comfort her

for just a moment before finishing her off as an act of mercy. She began to wail as he put an arm around her shoulder, and as the wail became a curse he pulled away from her just in time to avoid taking a filleting knife in the throat. The knife grazed the side of his neck, and scrambling back to his feet he renounced any hope of getting close enough to make contact between the pistol and her head. He fired a third time and was close enough to put it into her forehead, interrupting in mid-syllable a curse in Hungarian, or Lithuanian or Polish.

He stood over her weeping, disconsolate at her having proved him right. He dropped the pistol into the satchel and walked out the back door. The sky was brighter now, still overcast and dark, but the promise of the morning to come was there. None of the neighbors' lights were on, but he assumed he'd been seen.

*

He drove to the Sweet Cage to get Bill Gerard's car, on the assumption that the neighbors had probably heard the shot and that one of them might have had the presence of mind to take down the number of Betsy van Heuten's Mercedes. He hated to give up the Mercedes, and he considered switching the plates, but it would take time and he might be seen. It was just a two and a half or three hour ride down to the airport, anyway.

*

He parked the Mercedes next to the Lincoln and unlocked the side door with Sidney's keys. He moved through the dark to Renata's office where Bill's body lay.

The four ten lay on the desk with Amy Sue's blue panties still twisted, shimmering, around its barrel. Bill's keys were next to it, where Renata had dropped them. He placed them into his side pocket with his own and Sidney's. Hearing them clank, and feeling the jagged, unwieldy load cut into his thigh, he envisioned potential problems at the airport metal detector, and he pulled out his own key ring and tossed it onto the floor as the least useful set of the three. Not exactly a neat crime scene, he thought, with his keys on the floor next to the corpse, and his fingerprints all over a shotgun on the desk, but he didn't have time to dispose of any of it and in any case he'd be a distant memory by the time anybody found any of it and made sense of it all. In a way it struck him as funny.

*

He was pulling out of the driveway in Bill's Lincoln when he had second thoughts about Sidney's keys. They weren't just keys to the club, they were house keys and car keys, things he'd have a hard time replacing. It was no skin off his ass to swing by and drop Sidney's keys in his mailbox. Then he'd be on his way.

*

He got to Sidney's house and parked. He got out and put the keys in the mailbox and got back behind the wheel, then opened the door and got out again. There was no mail on Christmas, and Sidney would certainly need his keys long before he'd have occasion to check for mail. He took them out of the mailbox and walked across the crunchy snow of the lawn to the front door. The storm door was loose and he put the keys atop its knob so that they'd fall if the door was moved. He was halfway back to the car when the door opened and the keys fell with a light metallic smack.

'Charlie?'

'Oh, Sidney, yeah, I accidentally took your keys.'

'My keys?' Sidney squatted down and picked up the key ring. 'How'd that happen?'

'They fell onto the closet floor when I was hanging my coat up, and I picked 'em up, thought they were mine. You been to bed yet?'

'Why bother, the kids'll be up in an hour anyway. Thanks for bringing these back, I'd have been screwed without 'em '

'Well, Merry Christmas.'

'You too, Charlie.' Sidney turned and went inside.

*

He was beginning to feel tired, and for a minute he thought about driving out to the municipal airport in town and avoiding the drive, but here was one part of Vic's plan that did seem to hold water. If he did it, he'd be leaving a trail that would lead to him before he left New York, whereas it would ideally be several days at least before anybody could place him on a flight to New York that left a hundred fifty miles to the south. He took surface streets south and west toward the southernmost turnpike booth, an old habit he had to avoid paying thirty or forty cents extra on the toll. He took a short, impulsive two-block detour into a residential neighborhood as he neared an old girlfriend's apartment and slowed down to a stop in front of it. It was the end apartment of one of several identical red-brick buildings, cramped apartments in rows of four. He wasn't quite sure which of the buildings hers had been, and he didn't have the slightest idea what had become of her. In fact, he barely remembered anything about her beyond her name, what she looked like and where she had lived, but it seemed to him as he sat there that he'd spent some of the best nights of his life with her in one of these ratty little apartments. The buildings had deteriorated since he'd been there last, and in the dull haze of the morning he saw that wood was peeling off the front door of the nearest apartment in long, thin vertical spikes behind a torn screen door. He pulled away and headed again for the turnpike.

CHAPTER SEVENTEEN

The turnpike attendant was elderly and cheerful. 'Merry Christmas,' she said as she handed him his ticket. 'Looks like the snow's about done with.'

'Yeah, I hope so.'

'Going to see your family?'

'Uh-huh.'

'Well, you all have a nice holiday.'

'Thanks, you too,' he said, rolling the Lincoln's window back up. He rolled onto the turnpike and three miles later passed a sign informing him that he'd cleared the city limits. 'Never to return,' he added out loud. The surface of the road was slick but clear, without much accumulation, and he was able to drive over the speed limit without feeling in any danger of losing control of the Lincoln. The big car felt good and familiar. He was definitely missing the Mercedes, though, and he felt that unfaithful, guilty feeling again now that he was at the wheel of the trusty Lincoln, even though this one was Bill Gerard's and not his. Had been Bill Gerard's, anyway.

On the quiet, nearly empty road he realized that since he left the Sweet Cage he'd been riding in silence. He turned the radio on and switched around until he found a clear signal. It was another cowboy singer doing a Christmas carol and when he was done the adenoidal crime reporter was back on the job, reporting live from police headquarters. Charlie wondered what his hours must be like. He never heard anyone else doing the reports, and he never noticed their absence if and when the reporter was sick or took a vacation. Charlie listened with odd satisfaction as he joyfully detailed a brawl at a nude dancing establishment north of the city limits to which Sheriff's officers were called, without mentioning the Tease-O-Rama by name, then reported a Westside home burglary that might or might not have been his own at Bonnie's house. After that he went into some misdemeanor activity that didn't involve or interest Charlie. He didn't have anything to say about bodies being discovered anywhere yet.

He passed the first gas station of the trip and looked for the first time at the fuel gauge. It was moving toward the red, and he didn't know how soon he'd see another station open on Christmas, so he pulled into the center lane and turned off left onto the median. He parked next to a fuel pump, took a hundred-dollar bill from one of the rubberbanded stacks in the satchel and snapped it taut in his hands a couple of times, admiring the look and feel of it. He had been waiting a long time to spend some of this money.

There was no one in the station but the cash register operator, a pudgy, unhappy-looking young woman with short auburn hair and a pasty, junk-food complexion. 'Merry Christmas,' Charlie called out as he walked in. She looked dully at him without responding as he plucked a styrofoam coffee cup off a stack and poured himself a cup from a plexiglass pot.

He set the coffee down on the counter, followed by the hundred-dollar bill. 'Just the coffee, and I'm going to fill up on number seven out there.'

She pouted. 'I can't change this. Anyway, I don't have to. See that sign?' She pointed behind her at a sign on the wall:

NO 50'S OR 100'S ACCEPTED
AND NO CHECK'S

'Okay, how about this? Keep the change.'

She frowned, certain that something was wrong with the proposition. 'That'll be, like, ninety bucks.'

'Merry Christmas.'

'Yeah, you too,' she said, examining the bill. Once satisfied it was authentic, she turned the pump on for him. 'Thanks, mister. Your coffee's on the house.'

*

Back on the road he found the coffee helping somewhat, but he was still fading into drowsiness, despite the cold. He flipped the radio dial around and found much the same thing as yesterday, Christmas music and no talk programs. Unlike his company Lincoln, Bill's had a tape player, and he reached over and popped the glove compartment open. Inside were two tapes, *Have Yourself a Merry Little Christmas* and *Frank Sinatra's Greatest Hits, Vol. II*. He decided to stick to the radio.

At the second median rest stop he passed, the gas

station and restaurant were both closed, and he congratulated himself for having pulled over at the first. He began to feel stupid for having fully gassed up a car he was going to abandon, until he realized that he'd have had to spend a hundred on half or three-quarters of a tank, too.

Rows of bare, skinny trees lined both sides of this stretch of the turnpike. The sky was still grey, with patches of pale yellow in the distance, just above the horizon. A few stray flakes of snow lighted on the windshield from time to time, and Charlie took pleasure in the knowledge that after two or at most three days in New York, he'd never have to spend another hour in a cold climate again.

Two miles past the closed rest area he passed a recreational vehicle parked on the shoulder, its hazard lights flashing. An elderly man was peering into its engine, and a woman of the same age was standing next to him, her arms folded in front of her chest against the cold and looking as though she were about to cry. He felt bad for them, but he figured a Highway Patrol car would be along soon enough. He had a plane to catch.

*

A mile down the road, thinking of the frightened, desperate look on the old woman's face, he began to have doubts. He hadn't seen a state trooper since he started out. It was bitterly cold, and he knew damn well he could catch another plane if he needed to. He'd made it out of town, and now he could afford to be magnanimous.

What the hell, he thought, it's Christmas. He pulled

to the left and crossed the median at the next cop turnaround, with its threatening sign:

TURNAROUND FOR
HIGHWAY PATROL USE ONLY

He drove past them going the other way and was somehow gratified to see them still there. There were no more turnarounds until he got to the closed rest area, and he pulled into it and drove around the restaurant and back onto the southbound turnpike. Two miles later he pulled in behind the big, beige and white RV. The old man was still poking around under the hood, wearing a lumber jacket and a ratty toque.

'Having trouble?'

The man looked around the open hood at him. 'Goddamn thing's brand new, I can't figure out what the hell's wrong.'

'We're out of gas,' the woman said, her voice choking with reproach. 'You can't read a damn gas gauge, that's what's wrong.' The woman also had on a lumber jacket and a toque. 'Must've been ten, fifteen cars passed by since we pulled over, and not one of 'em stopped until now.'

'I could give you a ride to a gas station, except I don't know how close we'd find one open on Christmas. Have you got some kind of a siphon?' Charlie asked. 'I just filled up thirty miles back. Otherwise, I guess I could turn around and take you to the station back there.'

'We shoulda stopped when we passed it the first time,' the woman said. 'Like I told you.'

'I think I've heard about enough of that lip of yours.'

The man gave her a malevolent stare which seemed to have no effect on her at all. 'Yeah, I got a siphon. Go get it, Dot. You know where it is.'

The old woman climbed aboard the vehicle and the old man kept looking into the motor. 'Mind you, I'm not all the way convinced it's the gas. These new goddamn engines, no telling what's really going wrong with them.'

Dot returned momentarily with a rubber hose and a two-gallon metal gas can, and the old man took them around to the Lincoln while Charlie opened the gas tank. 'You need help?'

'I can siphon a goddamn gas tank just fine on my own. Thanks.'

As the man began sucking gasoline through the hose Charlie walked back over to where Dot stood. 'Sorry about Gunther. He just figures his Christmas is ruined.'

'That's okay. Where are you headed?'

'The wrong goddamn direction. He thinks he knows a road branches off just south of one of these exits we can take west and save some time. Well, maybe so, but what's the point of making time if you lose it all running out of gas?'

'That's true.'

'My first husband was a drunk and a liar, but he never ran out of gas as long as I knew him. I'm a registered nurse. I've always had to be responsible and on time, and I've never run out of gas in my life. But him—' She gestured contemptuously over her shoulder at Gunther, sucking and draining from the Lincoln into the gas can. 'I never met a man so full of shit in my entire life. Look at this goddamn thing. We can't near afford it, but there it is. Whatever possessed me to marry him I can't imagine.'

Gunther looked up, narrowing his eyes. 'What'd you say?'

'I said you're full of shit, you foolish old jackass.'

He snorted and went back to work.

'I'd invite you in out of the cold only it's a mess inside, and anyway he'll be done there in just a second.'

'That's okay,' Charlie said. 'How does that thing handle on ice?'

'Shitty. At least when Gunther's driving it. You know you got a cut on your neck?'

He put his finger to his neck where Renata had touched him with the filleting knife. He felt rough, pebbly dried blood, and when he pulled his hand away he saw that some of it was still glistening. 'Shaving. Did it shaving.'

Gunther stood up, having siphoned most of the can's capacity, and moved to the back to pour it into the RV's tank.

'I expect we'll have to drive all the way back to that first station,' Dot said. 'Won't be enough gas there to get this thing much further than that.'

'Gunther,' Charlie yelled. 'Take another canful if you need to.'

'Much obliged,' Gunther yelled back, and he took the empty can and the hose back to the Lincoln and began siphoning again.

'That's very kind of you, mister.' Dot shivered. 'I just don't know what possessed us to try to take off Christmas morning.'

North of them in the distance a car appeared, and as it drew nearer Charlie's sphincter tightened once again. It was a state trooper, and he was slowing down. As he pulled abreast of them, he came to a stop and his partner rolled his window down.

'You folks in some kind of trouble?'

'Not any more, officer. This young gentleman is letting us have some of his gasoline.'

'That thing doesn't run on diesel?'

'It's a gas model. Too damn hard to find diesel at the pump.'

The trooper in the passenger seat leaned out and looked at Gunther, who had the hose between his mouth and the Lincoln's tank. He looked up and without unpinching his lips gave the troopers a little nod and wave, signaling that all was well.

'All right, then. You folks have a merry Christmas, all right?'

Charlie and Dot nodded, smiling, and the troopers pulled back onto the road, the window rolling up.

Gunther finished filling the second can and headed to the back of the RV. He poured most of it in and climbed back aboard and tried to turn the engine over. It wheezed and clattered and didn't turn over.

'See? I told you it wasn't the goddamn gas.'

'Don't you know anything? Put a little in the goddamn carburetor.'

Gunther got out with the can, messed with the carburetor for a second, then emptied the remainder of the can into it. Dot looked over at Charlie, her arms still folded over her chest. 'He used to be a *policeman*. Can

you imagine? Never met a man so helpless in my life.'
Gunther retreated to the RV's cab. On his first try it
turned over and began rumbling steadily. He looked
down at the hood as if he didn't trust the motor to keep
running.

Gunther stuck his head out and yelled, 'Got 'er going.'

'Congratulations.'

'I'll just give it a minute or two here to warm up.'

'About a mile down the road there's a turnaround you
can use,' Charlie said.

'Thanks again.' Dot went around to the right side of
the RV and got back on board.

Charlie looked at them snapping at each other in the
cab, and he felt good. He had made a difference in their
lives. He started to get back into the Lincoln and realized
that he needed to go to the bathroom. He'd already lost
enough time without stopping again to take a leak. There
was a row of trees ten or fifteen feet back from the
shoulder, and he headed past the rear of the RV for it.

*

Behind the trees was a field, and in the distance he could
see a barn and what he thought was the roof of a house.
He let loose on a tree, watching the steaming flow arc
and splatter on the darkening bark. Now that he was a
free man, everything seemed different. He was intensely
aware of the smell of the urine, of the bark, and of smoke
from a wood fire. He zipped up, turned to face the
farmhouse and saw that there was indeed smoke rising
from the chimney. He walked clear of the row of trees
and past the rear end of the RV again, stopping to look at

something Gunther had had painted on it in large gothic script:

IT IS NOT THE END DESTINATION OF A
VOYAGE THAT MATTERS; IT IS WHAT ONE DOES
AND SEES ON THE WAY THERE.
DOT 'N' GUNTHER

So that's why these damn things are so slow, Charlie thought, and he was about to move on when the RV chugged without warning into reverse and its rear ladder smashed into his face, knocking him backwards onto the snow. A second later he felt the right rear tire going up against and then over his right arm, crushing it, and then over his chest, and his vision narrowed suddenly, going red and black around the rapidly closing border, and then it was gone.

*

'Jesus H. Christ, Gunther, you hit something big.' There was a second bump as the RV's back wheels rolled over a large object.

'The hell I did,' he snarled back.

'Stop and let's see what it is.'

Gunther resolutely ignored her and shifted into first. Again the RV lurched as it rolled forward over the thing.

'Goddamnit, stop. I'm getting out.' She opened her door and hopped out, hitting the snow at a slow run as the RV slowed.

'Woman, I've told you before not to get out before I bring this vehicle to a complete stop!'

She turned to Gunther, her voice rising. 'Oh, mercy. Oh, Gunther, you better get out. You run him over.'

The young man lay on the ground behind the RV, the aura of blood on the snow beneath him expanding around his chest. She reached for his wrist and felt no pulse, then pulled his right eyelid back to check his pupils.

*

Gunther stumbled over to her and stood over him. 'Is he dead?'

'He sure is.'

'Well, what the hell was the dumb bastard standing back there for?'

'Damned if I know.' She touched the collar of his overcoat. It was an expensive and warm-looking one, cut from some kind of thick, tweedy material. On his feet was a pair of highly shined burgundy wingtips. Dot's eyes moistened. The young man wasn't much older than her own son.

'What are we gonna do now?'

'Flag down those troopers, I guess, next time they pass.'

'Great. Just great. And I get into a whole shitload of trouble trying to explain how it happened. Lose my damn license, most likely.'

She reached into his pocket for his wallet. 'Let's see who he is . . .' There was no wallet, but there was a set of keys.

'Looks like the wallet's on his dashboard,' Gunther said.

He took the keys from her and unlocked the passenger side door. He pulled the wallet from the dash. 'Charles Lewis Arglist was his name. Member of the State Bar Association. Visa, Mastercharge . . .' He pulled the satchel off the seat and peered inside. Plane tickets, a .22 caliber pistol, a bottle of Johnny Walker and more money than Gunther had ever seen in his life. He took in a deep breath, let it out slowly, then snapped the satchel shut and calmly carried it back to the RV along with the wallet.

'There's a tarp up top of the microwave oven. Go get it.'

'What the hell for?'

He opened the satchel and showed her the contents. 'We're taking him with us.'

She stared at Gunther and the money for a moment, then turned her gaze back to the body on the ground. 'Good God, he must've robbed a bank.'

'Hurry up and get the tarp before someone drives by and sees him. And get me the shovel so I can move this bloody snow off into those trees over there.'

*

Half an hour later they were back at the service station filling up. The day was beginning to clear, and there were isolated, small swatches of blue among the clouds. Dot had scarcely spoken a word since they'd wrapped the body up and hidden it in the luggage bay, which was fine with Gunther. They would head back down south until they got to his westward shortcut, which led after fifty miles or so to an old quarry road. The quarry had been flooded for years and would hide the young man's body